ZERO IS THE KEY

Robert J. Guerrera

©2014 Robert J. Guerrera. All Rights Reserved

ISBN: 1502423693
ISBN 13: 978-1502423696

This is a work of fiction. Except in the case of historical fact, names, characters, places, and incidents either are the product of the author's imagination or are used fictitiously. Any resemblance to actual persons, living or dead, companies, organizations, events, or locals is entirely coincidental.

For Jeanine, Gavin, and Bryan

Acknowledgments

My most humble thanks and gratitude to my wife, Jeanine, for her sincere candor, invaluable insights, and selfless patience in contributing her ideas and editing expertise. Her love of languages and her linguistic talent allowed for an impartial and objective editor's eye throughout the writing process.

Thanks to my family and friends who have shared their support and encouragement. A heartfelt thank you goes to my brother for all of his encouragement and support throughout this project. To my mother, for her positive inspiration throughout my life.

Finally, I want to thank my children, Gavin and Bryan, for their patience during the past years. They were a willing and enthusiastic audience while I read the first draft to them. Their excitement about the story motivated me to see the project through to its fruition. Thank you.

Contents

1 The Mysterious Sinkhole 9

2 The Laboratory 22

3 On the Prowl 28

4 The Chase 37

5 Operation Gaul 47

6 Project Rainbow 68

7 Liber Abaci 80

8 Tachyons 93

9 Qarahunge 105

10 Cahokia 130

11 Temple of the Inscriptions 155

12 The Chosen 178

13 Amaru Muru 202

1 The Mysterious Sinkhole ✦

Munch, munch… The twins were devouring candy they had collected the night after Halloween.

Declan stared greedily at his sister's candy. "You going to eat those Pop Rocks?"

"How many times do I have to tell you to keep your thoughts, eyes, and hands off my food?" Dalya retorted.

Declan and Dalya had gone trick-or-treating at the usual time on Halloween night with their friends. The next evening, they decided to make a second round of candy collection in a clever attempt to acquire any leftovers from the Night of Spirits.

"Trick-or-leftovers," they yelled to the unsuspecting residents who opened the door to find two costumed youths eagerly waiting for sweet rewards to be thrown into their shabby paper bags. The twins ended the night with plenty of candy reaching the brim of their large bags. Declan dressed up as Indiana Jones, and Dalya dressed as a mountain climber, with ropes and clips wrapped around her body like coiled snakes. As the twins devoured their candy, the sun was beginning to set, radiating its colorful remnants of light before the star-filled sky approached. It signaled the siblings to go back to the house for dinner.

There was a forest that bordered the twin's property on three sides, surrounding the fifty-acre backyard. As the sun set, they noticed it. A strange, foggy light could be seen off in the distance deep in the forest. Greenish-blue rays poked through the many trees that surrounded the tree house the twins had built a few years ago. The mysterious light emanated its pulsating rays from an unrevealed location.

The athletic twins ran impulsively toward the light to find out what was happening. Panting, Declan arrived first at the light's source, almost falling into a hole. He twirled his arms in a backward motion, standing on one foot to regain his balance and to avoid falling into the awaiting pit. Dalya came upon the scene a few seconds later. She stopped and caught her breath, her long dark hair falling in front of her face. The hole was deep and about fifty meters in circumference. Peering down while lying flat on their stomachs, they noticed an object.

"Look, Dalya! There is some kind of rock down there."

"It looks like a meteorite!" Dalya responded.

"How long do you think it has been here?"

"By the looks of the soil's disturbance and resettling around the crater's ring, I estimate the time of the meteorite's entry to be around yesterday or the day before at the most," Dalya said, demonstrating a scientist's certainty. "However, the rock could simply be resting in a sinkhole."

"Sinkhole? What is a sinkhole?" inquired Declan.

"A sinkhole is basically formed through different

types of erosion. Cave walls or ceilings may collapse to form a hole. An underground water table could filter out the earth beneath a surface, which causes an area of soil to slowly or even quickly sink down to form a hole. Usually limestone rock is eroded away to form these pits. We have them here in the States, in places like Michigan, Kentucky, and Florida. They are found all over the world, too. Remember that cenote we visited when Mom and Dad took us to Mexico for summer holiday two years ago? We were hiking in the jungle, and you almost fell into the hole when you were taking pictures of it. Dad had to grab you by the hood of your rain jacket to keep you from falling in. Well, that was a sinkhole. It's like when you stand on the beach, and you feel the water taking the sand away from under your feet as the water retreats."

"Oh yes, I see what you mean. You know a lot about this subject."

Dalya grinned sheepishly, enjoying her brother's kind words. Her hazel eyes gleamed, and then she remarked, "The countries of Belize, Papua New Guinea, and Oman have really big sinkholes as well. Usually they are filled with rainwater like the one in Mexico. It's strange that this one is empty of water though." Dalya rubbed her right hand on her chin as she stared quizzically down into the hole.

Declan noticed how the glowing light reflected off his sister's long brown hair. Suddenly, the glow became brighter and a misty cloud of rays splayed toward them. Just then, a blinding light engulfed the unsuspecting onlookers, and in a few seconds all went dark in the hole.

"Wow!" the twins half whispered to themselves. They slowly turned their heads toward one another and stared into each other's glazed wide eyes, feeling scared and amazed at what they had just witnessed. Not many things caused the twins to be easily frightened; however, this strange event made them stir with discomfort. Realizing it was now twilight, the twins ran home through the blackening forest as the sky revealed the last remnants of sunlight between the silhouetted trees.

Declan's wiry muscular body moved quickly as he gasped for oxygen while running through the forest. "You think Mom and Dad will know we ate all of that candy before dinner?"

"Are you kidding? They know our Halloween routine. Remember last year when they caught us in our rooms late at night!" Dalya responded in a hoarse voice as she ran, her thin frame pumping alongside Declan. The twins ran the final hundred yards to the house as they cleared the forest. Two still, silent figures silhouetted by the living room lamp stood at the back entrance of the twins' home, observing them as they approached.

"Hi Mom and Dad!" the twins cautiously sputtered together. People always say twins do a lot of things at the same time spontaneously. The Salk twins were no exception. Their mom and dad stared at them with stern, thoughtful frowns.

"You missed dinner," Mrs. Salk pointed out.

Dad added calmly, "Go upstairs to your rooms and get ready for bed. We'll talk about this in the morning. By the way, next time no more candy before dinner...ever.

We'll also talk about why lots of candy is bad for your teeth and your health in general."

'Oh no, another speech looms over us about dental shame,' Dalya thought to herself.

✦

Bizarre sensations streamed though his body as Declan abruptly awakened from a deep slumber. A transparent milky mirage surrounded him. He rubbed his piercing green eyes and blinked several times to get rid of the morning's grogginess from his sluggish brain.

"Wow!" he whispered to himself, "This is an unusual vision." Declan changed from his pajamas into a pair of week-old jeans and an American flag T-shirt. He noticed that the translucent visions seemed to be accompanying his every motion as he puttered around his bedroom. That strange sensation inside his body felt like the slight queasiness one gets when one has just finished a roller coaster ride.

"Weird." Declan sighed, opened the curtains and windows to let some sunlight and fresh air into his unkempt bedroom. "Whoa!" he said loudly with fascination. "I am covered in some kind of soap-bubbled, milky shell. What is this? What is happening to me?"

After what seemed like a few minutes, the milky vision of his world seemed to partly vanish. The strange substance only outlined his body now. His books, baseballs equipment, Lego constructions, and other things were free from this strange apparition. The world looked nearly normal again compared to when he first woke up several minutes ago. Declan approached his full-body mirror, which hung beside the door. He anticipated a tired and disheveled boy peering back at him, but all he saw reflected was most of his messy room directly behind him. There was no Declan in the mirror. Not one square millimeter of himself or his clothing was revealed in the old, glass-smeared mirror. He stepped even closer, still there was nothing. Declan hesitantly inched closer to the mirror. Still, he was not present.

His pulse began to pound speedily in his temples. Declan felt nausea creep into his stomach and work its way up to his throat as he began to feel nervous. Placing his right hand on the mirror, he aggressively rubbed its surface until it unhooked and nearly crashed to the floor.

"Oh!" he uttered when he caught the mirror with both hands as it came within inches from hitting the wooden-paneled floor. Stabilizing the mirror, Declan drew a deep breath and then exhaled a warm blast of carbon dioxide onto the ornery mirror's surface. The gas and mirror performed the complex process of condensation.

Declan smiled with much relief. "I'm still here." Then he jumped, danced, turned, and contorted his body and limbs, expecting that maybe fast movements might be reflected by the reluctant mirror. Still, nothing of him was seen.

Dalya stood just inside the doorway. She was enthralled by her brother's spectacle and innocently giggled aloud. Startled, Declan jumped backward into the mirror and slammed into it. Shards of glass spilled onto the floor after a loud crashing sound boomed throughout the house. Mom and Dad were running errands in town, therefore he wasn't worried.

"What are you doing, crazy brother?" Dalya inquired, feeling amused.

"Oh, nothing. Just exercising," replied Declan, a bit irritated at his sister's tone.

"Exercising? Exercising for what, a role for a rodeo horse in a school play?"

"Something strange is going on. Come here to my clothing chest." He opened the old wicker storage chest and pulled out a round mirror with a long handle. "Look at my face, Dalya. It's not there!"

Dalya pressed her face close against the side of Declan's and saw nothing, not even her own face. "Wait a minute," Declan announced, "You have it too!"

"Have what?"

"A camouflage effect of some kind or a protective cover or something, like a shell that hides your image. See! We can't see your reflection either."

Dalya instantly grabbed the mirror and looked into it…nothing. With her right hand, she ran the mirror along her arms, hands, legs, feet, and every other part of her body that she should be able to see in the mirror. Still, there was nothing. Her body was hiding from her. Declan and Dalya tried other tools to investigate. Magnifying glasses, other mirrors of different sizes, water, and even drinking glasses were applied meticulously, but nothing worked. Still, the twins remained hidden.

Frustrated, the experimenters sat on Declan's floor. Disheartened, they quietly looked around; their eyes scanning the bedroom in quiet desperation for something, anything that might help them understand what was happening.

"Aha! I have an idea." Dalya jumped up and ran out of the room down the long corridor leading into her parents' bedroom. She reached into the bathroom's medicine cabinet and grabbed some talcum powder. Declan watched her reenter his room as she tightly held a large white plastic bottle in one hand while pointing at the bottle with her other hand. She gave a triumphant grin to Declan. She poured powder on one of Declan's arms and gleefully shouted, "Look! You can see an outline of your arm. Here, take some more." Dalya impulsively poured powder on Declan's head and the rest of his body. "Wow! This really works! I can see your shape now."

"Let me pour some powder on you." Within a few minutes, the twins were both covered on every square centimeter of their bodies. The siblings now stood in front of the bathroom mirror. Staring back at them were ghostly white figures. Dark spaces occupied the areas where their eyes, nostrils, and ear openings should be. Declan opened his mouth, seeing only a dark hole staring back at him.

"What is happening to us?" Dalya inquired.

"I don't know, sis, but we better find out."

✦

An hour had passed since their big discovery. Feeling befuddled, the twins tried to make sense of this surreal experience.

"So, I can see myself and my clothes. Everything appears normal except for this slight, white haze surroundding me. I can also see you, Dalya. You look normal to me. How am I to you?"

"It's the same for me, exactly like you just described. You look normal to me too. Let's go outside and see if others notice anything strange about us."

"Yes, and let's find anything that might help restore us back to normal," suggested Declan.

The twins lunged out of their house and walked into the surrounding grassy acreage. Both felt overwhelmed by the smells, colors, and sounds of the outdoors. Breakfast scents flowed from their neighbors' kitchens; various plant scents drifted through the air; freshly cut grass smelled more intense than ever before. The pines surrounding their property gave off their now powerful rich aromas. The California sunshine warmed their invisible bodies.

"I can smell more things and see farther than I ever have before," Dalya explained.

"I feel stronger and quicker too. I can also hear things from far away."

Just then, two wild street dogs ran swiftly toward them from a neighboring yard, barking and growling loudly. They must have seen them! Both Declan and Dalya crouched down as the large dogs lunged at them. In a flash, the twins sprang sideward as adrenalin poured through their blood vessels.

The two dogs became anxious and confused as they stopped in their tracks, looking for their targets. Determined, the canines jerked their heads around wildly, searching the air and sniffing the ground for the two undetectable humans. At a safe distance, the siblings waited while the dogs confusingly snapped their jaws, barked, and snarled into the air. After a few minutes, the twins relieved the dogs of their confusion and went on their way.

"It seems the dogs could see us when they first ran toward us. I thought we were invisible when we left the house," Declan said.

"Me too, but I think the invisibility changes randomly. On the street, we must have become visible at some point. Then, when we jumped aside, we must have become invisible again since the dogs couldn't find us."

Declan nodded. "Also, they were obviously unable to pick up our scent after we jumped aside."

The twins walked silently and pondered their situation, realizing how spectacular and special the invisible power could be. All of a sudden, out of nowhere—*Splash! Bang!* Water flung out from an opened front door followed by a large plastic bucket. The water and bucket fell onto the sidewalk just inches in front of the startled twins. A woman in one of the well kept suburban homes had emptied a bucket of stinky, mud-colored water onto the street, its contents splashing all over their clothing. The bucket had accidentally slipped from the neighbor's hands.

"Yuck!" Dalya blurted out as she stiffened her body, hands stretched out, feeling disgusted by the dirty water dripping from her skin and clothing.

"Nasty!" Declan added.

The woman walked out of her house to retrieve her bucket while singing a tune to herself. She didn't notice the twins standing right next to her and immediately returned to her abode.

"Gosh! We must still be invisible."

"I wonder when it stops, Dalya. We need to figure out when our invisibility switches on and off. Somehow, we are going to have to find a way to control this power." Declan wiped water out of his eyes.

They decided to return home. Visible once again, the twins walked along the sidewalk. *SCREEEEEEEEECH!* A flatbed truck honked, nearly running over the twins as they stepped of a curb to cross the street, lost in thought and conversation. Within a split second after the honking, both Declan and Dalya panicked and froze in place as the truck came barreling toward them. The young driver quickly braked hard to a full stop. He abruptly got out of his vehicle and ran toward the front of his large vehicle. Horrified, he expected two bodies to be lying on the ground. The young man anxiously peered over his hood. No one was there! The children had vanished.

Declan and Dalya remained quiet. Maybe they were afraid to receive a scolding from the driver about careless jaywalking. Or, the thought of being discovered might have alarmed them. Whatever the reason, they instinctively kept as quiet as a prairie dog hiding from a hawk.

The driver reached out his hand and grabbed at the empty space in front of the truck's grill. Scratching his head, he examined the ground at his feet. Quickly, he made a 360 degree turn, twirling on his feet, anticipating two injured children lying against a curb somewhere. He saw no one. The puzzled driver walked around the truck while eyeballing the pavement. He stopped, stared at the ground, and wondered where they had gone. Terror stricken, he slowly crouched down and peered under the vehicle, expecting two mangled bodies all bunched up under the old truck's carriage. He sighed with relief as the space revealed emptiness. Baffled, he shrugged and got back into his truck. Suddenly, he heard rocks and pebbles scuttling over the road nearby. Again, the driver jumped out of the truck expecting to see the children...still nothing. Wait! Did he see some transparent apparition pass in front of him like a mirage of water on a hot pavement's surface? Did he hear faded sounds of footsteps? No, impossible. It couldn't be. Again, he shrugged his shoulders, eased back into his truck, and drove on.

"Whew, that was close, Dalya."

"Gosh, I thought we were caught for sure." They stood three meters away from the near accident site and watched the truck disappear, swallowed up by the afternoon sunlight.

Dalya replied, "Let's analyze this problem for a minute. When the truck almost hit us, and also when those dogs came at us, I instantly felt startled and scared all at once. Did you feel that way also, Declan?"

"No, not at all. I wasn't scared of the dogs."

"Declan, I know you too well, brother. Tell me the truth," Dalya prodded. "Weren't you scared, even just a little bit?"

"I guess just a little bit."

"Just a little bit, Declan?" Dalya said in her authoritative, persistent tone.

"Well, all right. Those dogs really scared me," Declan finally confessed with a slow release of breath, feeling defeated in revealing the truth.

"You see what is happening, Declan?"

"Yeah, we become invisible when fear and stress are triggered within us."

"Right, I come to the same conclusion! So, we need to control this power. We don't want to be talking with Mom and Dad or our friends when all of a sudden we disappear in front of their eyes because something startles us. Mom would freak out, and I don't know how Dad would react," Dalya said, feeling alarmed.

"I know how he would react. He would be very excited and ask us a bunch of questions. Dad would want to know how this power works. He would be like a mad scientist."

The wheels of Dalya's mind were turning like gears in a grandfather clock. She suggested, "Why don't we go down to my basement science lab? We can experiment and test different ways to make ourselves disappear and reappear again."

"Great idea!"

2 The Laboratory ✦

Plop, plop. Low hums and other sounds gurgled from the busy, dusty basement. Four tiny windows reluctantly allowed the sun's rays to sneak into the room. After months of visiting garage sales, mail ordering through catalogs, and collecting discarded things from the local middle and high schools, Dalya and her Dad had meticulously constructed a state-of-the-art science lab, according to an eighth grader's standard. Her parents donated two long sofas, a coffee table, and some standing lamps for one corner of the basement, which gave the room a cozy feeling. With his large carpenter's hands, Dad constructed some large wooden shelving units and tables for Dalya to conduct her experiments.

The lab's walls were nearly covered with shelves full of science books, pamphlets and Dalya's experimental notes. Plenty of supplies and equipment, such as compounds, beakers, trays, sponges, wire mesh, test tubes, rubber seals, heating forks, Petri dishes, tuning forks, magnets, goggles, scales of all kinds, wires, batteries, and Bunsen burners could be found to carry out Dalya's experiments.

"I remember when you started the project. You

bothered Mom and Dad for weeks to get them to give up the basement for the lab. It seems like yesterday since you began. What's that bubbling over there?" Declan asked, pointing to a table with a flask filled with a blue jelly-like chemical foaming at the top.

"You haven't been down here in a while, have you? I've set up some new experiments. That one over there is an experiment I'm conducting to develop an immediate clothing stain remover. The idea is rub the solution on your clothes like this," Dalya patiently demonstrated. She used a spatula to scoop some hot goo out of the flask and spread it on a piece of white scrap cloth with an orange stain. Within three seconds, they witnessed the stain lightening up a bit and then the clothing scrap caught fire. "Shoot!" the young scientist blurted loudly. Dalya quickly released the fabric and it fell to the floor. Immediately, she snuffed out the fire with her shoe.

"Still need to perfect that process," Dalya mumbled to herself. "Also need to figure out a way for the goo to be used at a safe temperature, besides just hot. It must be bottled, shelved, and used safely. I'm getting closer to finding an answer to the problem."

"Why do you keep the lab so dark these days?" Declan surveyed the busy, crowded lab.

The basement was dimly lit by soft bulb lamps and neon colors emanating from various experimental centers on the tables around the room. "I want it dark so that I can quickly spot any slight changes in the flasks. I can then observe significant variations in my experiments, which would allow me to make any necessary adjustments to the potions. A small change in the shade of a liquid's color or the tone and pitch of a sound cannot go unnoticed. I could miss an opportunity to solve a problem or pass over an important new discovery. Besides, I concentrate better in the dark using my special headlamp."

Dalya approached another table. "With this experiment, I'm trying to reproduce the northern lights. Maybe I can figure out a way to improve radio communications in the Earth's atmosphere by harnessing the northern lights' energy source and then bottle it up to give it to the military. They could then develop spyware to block radio and satellite communications from foreign enemies."

The twins quietly and slowly walked around the room as Dalya explained her other experiments in an animated yet controlled voice.

"In that corner over there, I'm investigating tornadoes with sand-blowing machines and vacuums that I rigged up."

"Why's that?"

"Well, tornadoes could also be a big source of energy. Imagine if we could create one of these in a special building and somehow suck the energy from it to make power. We could turn the tornadoes on and off with a switch whenever we needed them. Wouldn't that be an accomplishment?"

"Yeah, it sure would." Declan felt amazed and proud of his sister's scientific knowledge.

"Now, how shall we approach our invisibility

problem?" Declan inquired.

"I have some ideas." Dalya explained in detail how the invisibility could be controlled. "We should build a special electromagnetic field that we could turn on anytime to make ourselves invisible. The magnetic field would make whatever is connected to us also invisible."

Declan's interest peaked, and he excitedly contributed some ideas. Dalya tinkered with her equipment while Declan hastily scribbled down notes. His hand became sore from the intense writing. After a while, Declan held up the notebook with diagrams. He added, "The gadget could look like this. It would have an on/off button to make us disappear and reappear whenever we wanted."

"Excellent idea," Dalya said approvingly. "The gizmos could be placed on our wrists like bracelets. They could even be voice activated!"

Just then, they heard someone sneeze outside one of the lab's windows. A rose bush shook. The twins froze with fear, stood silently, and stared at each other. They both noticed one of the windows leaning outwards behind the thick, brown, dusty curtains.

Declan yelled, "Is that you, Artemis Griswald, sticking your nose in our business again?"

Then the twins heard footsteps moving quickly away from the lab. Without saying a word, the siblings closed the window and began to construct the important gizmo.

Several hours later, Mom and Dad called for dinner. The twins unwillingly went upstairs to eat. They inhaled their food, dismissed themselves, and ran back down to the basement to continue working. At around midnight, Mom came down. "Darlings, it's nearly midnight. You should go to bed now."

"Mom, I'm working on my science fair project for Mr. Tesla. Declan is helping me. Can we stay up since it is Saturday night?"

Mrs. Salk gave in. "Oh, I guess that will be fine, darling. But get to bed soon, will you? Good night, you two."

"We will. Good night, Mom," both responded in harmony. The twins tinkered, welded, and crafted on the contraptions until the morning sunrise. Finally, they stumbled upon a way to successfully rig the gizmos with an effective on/off button. After even more tinkering, they accidentally discovered a way for the gizmos to work by the two voice commands *invisible* and *return*.

"Done!" cheered Dalya.

"All right, ready?" asked Declan nervously.

"Yeah," said Dalya. "Invisible!" she commanded. Dalya vanished.

"It works, Dalya!"

Then she commanded, "Return!" Dalya reappeared.

Declan made the same commands to his gizmo. It also functioned well.

"Wow, I cannot believe we did it, Declan. Our machines work!" The experimenters hugged each other in triumph.

The twins were now ready to become invisible anytime they wanted.

"I couldn't say how we made these machines work.

If someone asks, I couldn't explain it, Dalya."

"Neither could I. We just got lucky, I guess.

"That's for sure," Declan agreed.

Declan smiled at his sister and hysterically exclaimed, "We are now the luckiest people on Earth!"

Or were they? Other interested parties would want to be lucky also…and they would have other, more sinister intentions with this new and incredible power.

3 On the Prowl ✦

A tall, slender man led a scientific team to the forest where the twins had found the mysterious hole. Men and women with sophisticated equipment and sniffing dogs were busy searching the forest. The entire area had been secured and was guarded by heavily armed military personnel. The public was not permitted to see the activity taking place around the pit. Scientists examined, measured, and took samples of every surrounding tree's branches, leaves, and bark. Soil was carefully collected and placed in special clear bags labeled *Confidential*. Insects, small animals, and trash were diligently collected and placed into special air-tight containers stored in vans to be whisked away to some secret location.

A week had passed since the investigators had arrived and still they had not found anything significant. A day after the twins left the hole, the soil completely caved in because of a heavy evening rain. The wet mud layered itself and filled up the whole like a cement truck that had poured its thick contents onto a new road. The tall man hurriedly walked around barking orders at people while his key chain swayed and banged loudly against his hip. His team of specially trained government scientists called SOUP, which is an acronym for *Scientists Of Undercover Projects*, had already known about and found several more of these mysterious holes, which had opened up in different locations around the world.

The SOUP agents were puzzled about this particular hole because of light tremors that regularly shook the forest's topsoil. The scientists' detection instruments and seismographs couldn't pinpoint the exact location of the tremors so they were unable to find the source of them. The elusive hole hid well from the uninvited intruders until one night a young female SOUP agent stepped unexpectedly into some quick soil, a combination of mud and soil that behaves like quicksand.

"I found something," she shouted to her fellow agents. Despite its name, quick soil usually swallows its victims slowly, but this was no ordinary mud. The woman sank about twenty centimeters per minute. "Help me, someone. I'm sinking fast!" she now yelped. Agents came and pulled her out with their long poled metal detectors.

A small fleet of special vacuum trucks were brought in. The vehicles sucked all of the mud and soil out of the hole until they could see the bottom. Emptiness stared stubbornly back at them.

"You may want to see this!" The young woman was now crouching down at the rim of the hole. "A few smeared footprints next to this Halloween candy wrapper…Children!"

"Since there are only two different sets of footprints, it seems that there were only two of them, enjoying their candy without anyone else knowing. Given the shoe sizes, they are probably middle-school aged children or older," added the leader convincingly.

"Well, at least one of them is a girl," the woman said as she carefully picked up a necklace of fake red gems and diamonds.

The tall man gave a satisfying grin. SOUP scientists are also trained to be astute detectives since their job was to investigate, analyze, and document unexplained occurrences in the world. Paranormal events were their specialty. SOUP could learn a great deal from unusual events and report its knowledge to the highest levels of the government and military. Powerful weapons could be made. Thumper guns, ray guns, sound guns, and other secret military devices were all things made as a result from SOUP's successful investigations. Another part of the job was to protect their secret knowledge. Espionage was a constant worry.

After some time, the leader figured out which street the sinkhole discoverers lived on. Keys dangling against his jeans, he briskly walked toward a house and rang the doorbell. Mrs. Mortimer came to the door and politely greeted the stranger. After a few questions, she pointed to a house. "That one over there with the wrap-around porch at the end of the cul-de-sac bordering the forest."

A minute later, the keys went silent. The SOUP leader stood on the identified front porch and waited for someone to open the door and greet him. He knocked a second time while ringing the bell impatiently. The agent began to feel irritated. No answer. It was Saturday, so the residents must be on a family trip, grocery shopping, or taking care of errands. When he received a call about the sinkhole, he scrambled down the steps and drove off in his black truck. The unmarked vehicle's engine roared at full speed. "I'll return soon," the agent promised to himself.

✦

"You're listening to the Top 40 Billboard radio hits from KFRC Santa Mahara," blasted a man's voice from Declan's radio headphones.

"Declan, lunch is ready. Your favorite! Peanut butter and jelly sandwiches are waiting on the dining room table for you. Grab Dalya, will you!" ordered Mom.

Dad, Mom, and the twins all sat at the table. Northern California shared another beautiful, sunny Saturday with its residents. Observant swallows perched nearby while the family enjoyed the sandwiches. Silently, they peered out the big French doors, observing their large backyard. At the end of their property's fields, pine trees swayed from a strong breeze, like synchronized swimmers flexing their limbs in perfect form.

The blue autumn sky remained clear, kicking out any clouds that tried to invade its space.

"Do you have water polo practice today, Declan?" asked Dad.

"No, Dad. Coach cancelled today because his little boy is sick. Since Mrs. Douglas is out of town, he's taking care of Timmy."

"When is your next game?" inquired Mom.

"Oh, not until two weeks from now. We play *The Marlins* from Hodesta."

"Dalya, how is your science fair project coming along, honey?" Dad asked.

"Very well, I think. My project is about the unusual behavior of fire. I am going to present a report on spontaneous combustion. It is about people who suddenly explode and catch fire. I find this very fascinating. There must a scientific explanation for this phenomenon."

"Really?" Dad raised his eyebrows. "What if there isn't?"

"There always is, Dad. Also, I am writing a report on fire tornadoes."

"Wow!" Mom and Dad blurted at the same time.

"Those things really exist?" Mom asked.

"Yes, they do. Over fifty fire tornadoes have been documented around the world.

Currently, I'm making an experiment to show how these hot twisters work. I built two different machines featured in *The Young Scientist* magazine. They can replicate various flame movements."

"What a wonderful project. Is that why I've heard so much banging around and other sounds coming out of the cellar last week?"

"That's right, Dad."

Dalya began to feel tense.

"We would love to see your work when it is all finished!" Mom said proudly.

"Sure, that would be…fine…Mom."

Declan now entered the conversation. "I've helped Dalya so she can finish before the due date. That way we'll have time to properly test the machines to make them ready for the science fair." Declan hoped his remark would end their discussion on the topic.

"If you need any help, let me know, since I build things all the time at work. I'd be happy to help you, honey." Dad gave Dalya an affectionate look while softly clutching her shoulder with his large hand.

"Thanks, Dad, but Declan and I can handle things." She sat quietly for a minute and pondered something. "You know, Dad, there is something else you could help us with sometime."

"Uh, we'll come to you when we are ready, Dad," Declan interrupted, giving a quick glance of disapproval to his sister.

"Is everything all right, son?" asked Mom, feeling suddenly concerned.

Declan started to feel a bit tense. "Yeah, we'll let you know soon." The parents shot each other a quick worried glance across the dining table.

"All right," Mom responded suspiciously. Declan realized that his body was beginning to fade slightly. His limbs took on a milky white color. He was turning invisible right in front of his parents. The conversation had made Declan feel nervous and tense. His body responded by pumping adrenalin through his veins as part of the fight-or-flight syndrome. He and Dalya wanted nothing more than to finish eating and to retreat to the basement. Declan cautiously glanced at Dalya and realized she was terrifyingly aware of his metamorphosis.

'Trouble,' he thought. 'My parents are going to freak out if they notice this.'

"Finished! I'm going to my room now. See you later."

Declan jumped out of his chair and bolted upstairs to his bedroom. Confused, Mom and Dad stared at Declan as he exited the dining room. The rest of the family finished lunch and cleaned the dishes. Mom had a special Saturday seminar to teach Latin linguistics at the local university. She had only been a professor at the school for three years when she was promoted to lead the Ancient Languages Department. They all said their goodbyes as Mom darted out of the house to get to the university on time. Soon after, Dad left the house to check on his workers' progress at a large construction site. The twins decided to go out into the neighborhood to try their new invention outside of the lab.

A black unmarked car wound its way around the sleepy suburb where the twins were experimenting with their gizmos.

"Invisible!" commanded each sibling.

The gizmos dutifully responded and concealed the twins from the rest of the world. Just seconds after, the stealthy government issued-car hummed its engine, passing unaware a few feet away from the twins. The vehicle braked, hesitated, and then turned around the corner onto the next street.

"Return!" commanded each twin at the same time. Magically, they reappeared to the world.

"Now I think our next step is to adjust the gizmos to also respond to whispered commands, Declan." They rushed back to the laboratory and tinkered until the gizmos would reliably react to whispers as well.

✦

"All right, the machines respond well to our whispers. Let's go celebrate our success with some snacks and a Big Slurp Cola at the Dribbling Dan. What do you think, Dalya?"

"Good idea, brother. Let's go!" The pavement warmed up from the autumn sun as the afternoon approached. Local teenagers cruised and skidded around the streets in their muscle cars. Music blared for the whole neighborhood to hear. The twins arrived at the convenience store's small parking lot when suddenly a burly teen barreled out of the entrance.

A clerk desperately shouted, "Come back here, thief. Bring those cigarettes back, ya hear! Help, help me someone!"

Instantly, Declan commanded, "Invisible!"

He vanished and waited for the shoplifter, the infamous local bully named Isak. Isak was one of the toughest and meanest guys in the neighborhood. He was known for being fierce with anyone who didn't do what he wanted. If one didn't give him his pocket change or didn't do what was told, he would find himself under the pounding fists of Isak. If one had a bruised face or a black eye, the other neighbor kids would ask if one suffered from the inevitable *Isak's attack*, since hardly anyone on the block escaped from it. There was a certain rhyme to it and the claim was used by all of the kids.

As Isak darted toward Declan, the twin stuck his foot out. The bully, who was running at full speed, toppled over, spilling his sweater's contents. Isak hit the pavement face-first, followed by the rest of his body.

"Oomph! Darn it!" He got up and was ready to run off again when a powerful blow struck him in the stomach. "Oh!" he gasped while breath left his body. Isak went down on all fours just inches away from the invisible Dalya. By this time, the short, wiry Asian man who worked in the store and two bystanders firmly grabbed Isak and escorted him back to the Dribbling Dan.

Isak's face displayed a bewildered look about the whole episode. "What the heck?" he mumbled as the three men brought him back to the convenience store. Moments later, he was whisked away by the police.

"Nice work, brother."

"Thanks for the help. I could get used to being invisible. A lot of good could come from it."

The twins ducked behind a hedge and both then commanded softly to their gizmos, "Return!"

Visible again, they proceeded with their initial plan to purchase their well-deserved drinks and snacks. They swallowed their Big Slurp cokes and devoured donuts while they walked home in a carefree and proud state of mind.

4 The Chase

"Twins are a unique type of people," Dalya informed her friend Penny in her biology class. She and her lab partner had finished their assignment early and were cleaning up their work area while the other students in the class were still laboring away at their intricate experiments.

"How's that?" asked the curious pigtailed girl.

"Well, one out of every hundred couples will have twins. And there are two types of twins, too, fraternal and identical." Dalya was taking it upon herself now to educate her lab partner and best friend. "My brother and I are fraternal."

"What's the difference?" Penny inquired.

"Well," Dalya now had her scientific instructional voice in place, "Twins are identical if they come from a mother's single egg. Once it is fertilized, it divides itself into two identical eggs. Each egg then grows into a separate human being. Bingo! Two identical twins are born. The mother gives birth to two babies instead of one!"

"Can an egg divide into more than two?"

"Sure. The egg that is fertilized can split into three

eggs which can form three human beings called triplets. Four eggs are quadruplets and so on."

"Wow! What are the chances of triplets and quadruplets being born?"

"Triplets occur in one out of every five hundred thousand births, and quadruplets happen in about one in every 729,000 births. Now, my brother and I are from two separate eggs which our mom's body produced right from the start."

"So, you two didn't come from one egg," Penny affirmed, showing her understanding.

"That's right."

"But you and Declan were born at the same time."

"Yes. Twins are usually born just minutes apart. For example, Declan and I were born twenty minutes apart but on separate days."

Penny's eyebrows had risen in surprise. "What do you mean?"

"You see, Declan was born at 11:50 p.m., just before midnight. I was born at 12:10 a.m., just after midnight the next day. He is older by twenty minutes and born the calendar day before me. My mom says Declan was born on a Thursday night and I on Friday."

"Aha," Penny blurted out, her brain satisfied with Dalya's answer. "I've heard stories about twins being extra close, having their own secret language. Is this actually true?"

"Well, yes it is. Growing up, Declan and I had our own sign language when we played together. This secret communication is known as twin talk." Dalya moved her hands and fingers around to show different symbols she and Declan had used in the past. "Also, we were in tune with each other. If one of us felt happy or sad, the other would know somehow. It's almost like we could read each other's minds sometimes."

"Wow! Amazing yet freaky!"

"You could say that twins are best friends. I know that Declan and I are really close and trust each other like best friends do."

Just then, the twin froze as a thought stormed into her mind. A rushing pulse shot up to Dalya's temples as adrenalin raced through her body.

"Dalya, are you all right?"

Penny looked concerned.

Suddenly, Dalya's body began to fade into a transparent haze. Penny's eyes widened and her mouth dropped open in surprise. Dalya could see her hands and arms begin to fizzle out. She abruptly brought her arms under the table and then hunched down, quietly muttering the command into her gizmo that was wrapped around her left wrist under her long sleeved sweater. Within a second, her arms and hands magically solidified again.

"Oh…my…word!" whispered Penny in disbelief. "You looked shocked all of a sudden, and your body began to disappear."

Dalya took a deep breath and exhaled. "Did anyone else notice?"

"I don't think so. Everyone is still busy doing experiments."

"I have to go now. Can we talk later?" Dalya gathered her things without waiting for Penny's answer.

The near-panicked twin hurriedly packed her school books, raised her hand, and asked, "Mr. Tesla, can I go? I'm not feeling well. I think I ate some bad food during lunch. Penny has our finished lab report."

"Yes, no problem. Are your names on the report?"

"Yes, they are, sir."

"Hope it wasn't our infamous cafeteria food. Feel better soon."

"Penny, we'll talk later." Dalya bounced out of her seat and nearly sprinted out of biology class, leaving behind her bewildered friend. Cruising impatiently down the school hallway, Dalya jammed her right hand down her front jeans pocket. She unfolded a note with their birthdays scribbled on it. Below were the words *for your eyes only*.

"I must meet Declan as soon as possible. We must analyze this message," she whispered to herself.

✦

Declan was already in Dalya's basement lab. He left school before the last bell rang because his sports period ended twenty minutes early as the teacher had to attend to an injured boy who sprang his ankle during the basketball lesson. Declan slipped out of the gym unnoticed. Dalya entered and found him closely observing a smudge on one of the small windows covered with old curtains.

"Hey!"

"Whoa!" Declan jumped, startled. "You scared me, sis!"

"What's up, Declan?"

"I think somebody tried to spy on us through the window. Look at this impression on the glass. See that?" Declan pointed to the smeared spot with his pinky finger.

"Yes, I do."

"The smudge definitely looks like a nose print and these smaller ones are from fingers pressed against the glass," Declan explained. Both grew silent in thought.

"Who would be spying on us?" Dalya asked. "Do you think somebody knows about our secret?"

"It's very possible."

"Look at this, Declan." Dalya unrolled a paper and handed it to her brother.

He studied it for several minutes. "Birthdates...*eyes only*...what is this? Hmmmm. Perhaps this is some kind of secret message." Wide-eyed, Declan slowly looked up from the small piece of paper. "Someone has probably written a coded message to us! Where did you get this, Dalya?"

"Found it in my school locker this morning. I just placed it in my pocket and forgot about it since I was in a rush to get to first period on time. But, I remembered during last period."

"There must be a connection with our birthdates and there's probably more to what is written here. We do not have enough information to make any sense of the message. Let's put some of your detective chemical solution on this paper and see if the fluid makes any additional hidden writing appear. Maybe we'll get a more complete picture of what's on this paper."

After they carefully brushed the detective fluid on the secret document, the twins were ready to inspect it. The solution worked. A letter formation slowly became visible before their eager eyes. All twenty-six letters of the alphabet were jumbled up randomly in a snake-like shape. The letters lay side by side, one by one, in faded script. Declan and Dalya huddled over it in the darkened cellar lab.

"Look, Dalya. It is possible this coded text can be figured out based on your birthday. I think the day of your birthday shows how many letters one skips while reading this message. Maybe our birth month August indicates the starting point. That means we begin on the eighth coded letter of this snake letter formation. The second coded letter will be fifteen spaces counted forward, according to the fifteenth, your actual calendar birthday in August. We'll write down every letter using this method. Then we can figure out what words the letters will spell. We'll know the message is complete when no more words can be deciphered."

"What makes you so sure about using my birthday and not yours since we were born on two different days?"

"It's just a hunch. The message was delivered to your locker and not to mine. Therefore, it is more likely your birthday will work. The Saturday night television series *Thinking Thieves* featured something like this once. If your birthday doesn't work, we could try mine. Maybe my hunch will work. Let's give it a go, shall we?"

After about twenty minutes, they had written down various words and sentences. Dalya read aloud the first part of the message. "*Dear Dalya. We must meet right away. You and your brother are in danger. Trust me when I say that I am your friend and will try to protect you.*"

Dalya continued with fascination, "The second coded phrase reads *Time flies with jet wings*. The third group of deciphered words reads *Gustav's tall construction*. The fourth message reveals the words *Enter second stage*. The last sentence says *Once you and Declan are there I will contact you*. That's all there is."

"Whoa!" Both of them blurted loudly, feeling astonished. Just then a thump followed by some tapping sounded from the far cellar window.

"Let's go, Dalya!" Declan ran across the lab, up the stairs, and shot out the back door. Dalya sprinted quickly to catch up to him. Down the lane leading away from their backyard, the twins could see a black-hooded figure feverishly pedaling a bicycle. "Someone's definitely been spying on us, Dalya." Running to the open garage, they found their motocross bicycles and sped off to catch the hooded intruder.

The person turned onto a small dirt path leading into the woods. Pumping hard, Declan pushed ahead of Dalya, until he disappeared into the thick brush. The path narrowed, squeezing the bikers in its tight grip. They rode downhill, then uphill, winding right and left. The bikers swerved around potholes and large rocks. They hopped and jumped their bicycles over large tree branches lying across the path.

Several seconds later, Dalya saw a clearing up ahead where two bikes lay tangled together in a heap. *Oomph, oh!* Dalya heard gasps and grunts from two people on the ground who were engaged in a physical struggle. She heard fists hitting bone followed by thudding and muffled sounds. Dust kicked up around the two entwined bodies. Instinctually, Dalya pressed her gizmo button.

"Hey, what the...?" cried the biker as an invisible force shoved him off of Declan. He stood up in startled amazement.

Then his stomach caved in, and his head and body jerked forward as he fell hard to the ground. In a flash, Dalya had punched him in the stomach and then kicked him on the back. He lay lumped on the dusty forest path, hyperventilating from the bike chase and struggle.

Declan sensed that Dalya was around and kept quiet to keep her invisibility a secret. Dalya was thin and small boned, but her martial arts skills were effective after three years of training.

Declan slowly walked over, still breathing heavily, and flipped back the intruder's hood to reveal the culprit. "Jules, what's going on?"

"Wait a minute, Declan!" Jules' eyes were wide-open. "How did you move so quickly to knock me down?"

"I've got lightning speed," Declan answered dismissively. "Why are you spying on us, Jules?"

"Someone paid me to do it. Somebody wants to find out what you and your sister are working on."

"Who paid you?"

"I don't know."

"What do you mean you don't know?"

Suddenly, the ninth grader leaped up and started running away. Before he could acquire a full sprint, Dalya tripped and pushed him down. Jules landed head first onto the pine-needled floor. Declan caught up to them and stood over Jules. Confused, the boy looked up at Declan.

"I have lightning speed, remember? Now, who is it, Jules?"

"Like I said before, I don't know. It's the truth. I received a note in my mailbox with twenty dollars. It said to observe you and report back by written letter to a post office box address. I would make twenty dollars or more per letter depending on how much information I would write back to them. That's all, man, I swear," Jules confessed between his gasping breaths.

"Where's the address?"

"I'm not sure. The address changes every week."

"Give me the last one." The twin quickly searched through the ninth grader's sweater and jeans pockets while Jules half-heartedly resisted. "All right, here we are." Declan opened up a small white piece of paper that had been meticulously folded several times. There was no letter or address, just a girl's name with a smudged phone number. He eyed Jules hard, and Jules anxiously lied, "I threw it away as I was told to do."

Just then, Declan felt a finger tap his right shoulder. He turned around and saw Dalya holding up another piece of paper. The downed figure was unaware of the discovery. Dalya had found the paper a few meters away under some scattered pine needles near the bicycles. It must have fallen out of Jules's pocket during the struggle. Turning away from Jules, Declan secretly read the note. *Spy on the Salk twins and find out what they are working on. Report back and we'll let you know how to contact us.*

"Oh boy," Declan mumbled to himself under his breath. He approached Jules to address him. "You can go. If we catch you again around our property, we'll call the police and tell them you are trespassing. Dalya lifted your fingerprints from our window to use as evidence. The police will believe us and put you in jail. Get out of here, now."

"But how will I get home? You trashed my bike when you crashed into me."

"Use that spy money you made to catch the bus or walk home. Maybe you can pay for bike repairs too. See you later, spy."

Feeling defeated, Jules got up and slowly walked away with his head down. After some time, the road swallowed the dark figure in the far distance.

A lone bicycle pedaled next to Declan. Dalya reappeared.

"Thanks, sis," Declan said proudly.

"You're welcome, brother."

5 Operation Gaul ✦

Knock, Knock, Knock. A man waited for the front door to open. Nearly two months had passed since the sinkhole discovery. During this time, SOUP had been closely watching the family and decided to wait patiently before making any effort to capture the siblings. They needed to know if other people were involved with the twins. The door abruptly opened. It was Mrs. Salk.

"Hello, can I help you?"

"Uh yes, I hope so. My name is Frank Fermi," he lied. "I am with the Santa Mahara Gas and Electric Company." He brandished a fake employee ID from his wallet.

"We are going to install some gas and electric lines underground and would like you to be careful traveling on your street for the couple of weeks."

"Oh, all right. Thank you for informing us."

"Do your children walk to school using the road in this direction?" He pointed down the street.

"Yes, they do."

"Which grade are they in?"

"Is that information important?" She glared at the man.

"No, it is not. I apologize," he replied, revealing a fake smile. "All right, please let them know to be careful in the coming weeks. There will be lots of holes and exposed gas lines. For safety reasons, may I check your gas meter and inspect your yard around the house? We are checking every house here in the vicinity to make sure your current gas lines are able to accommodate the new ones."

"Um, no problem. You can enter the backyard through our fence over there."

"Thank you, it will just take a few minutes."

The agent walked slowly around the perimeter of the home pretending to inspect the ground, cables, and the gas meter in the back yard while sneaking glances into the home's windows. After several minutes, the agent finished his inspection and seemed satisfied with his observations.

"Have a good day, Mrs.…?"

"Salk, Margaret Salk."

"Take care, Mrs. Salk. Thank you again." The man's keys jingled as he stepped off the front stairs and climbed into his disguised repair van splashed with the city's name and logo. He slowly drove off. Margaret watched him drive away.

It was two weeks before the Christmas holiday began. The Salks were able to get permission to leave school for an extended holiday; there was a fictitious family emergency regarding Mrs. Salk's family in France. The twins would have no problem in making up their school work once they returned.

She returned to finish her packing for the family's three-week European holiday trip. She wanted to have an easy morning tomorrow without all of the last minute packing and rushing around.

✦

The twins puzzled over the mysterious riddle they had decoded.

"I've got it!" said Declan. "*Time flies with jet wings* means to fly in an airplane."

"Right! And *Gustav's tall construction* must be the Eiffel Tower! Gustav Eiffel is the original designer and builder! *Enter second stage* must mean the second part of the Eiffel Tower's construction."

"I remember something Dad described to me once, Dalya. He told me the tower's construction was managed in different stages. The first stage refers to completing construction until the first balcony. The second stage to the second balcony, and so forth. *Enter second stage* means we are to meet someone at the second balcony."

"Let's get back to the house and ask when exactly we'll visit the Eiffel Tower while we are in Europe. It must be the meeting point. Whoever wants to talk with us must know about our family trip to Europe," explained Dalya.

They didn't notice the disguised repair van parked down the street as they walked home from school.

✦

Early the next morning, it was still dark outside and very quiet. With the family Volvo loaded with medium-sized backpacks stuffed to the limit, they puttered off to the San Francisco airport.

Five minutes didn't even pass when an unmarked van pulled slowly up to the house, its low engine humming quietly to not attract any attention. Headlights turned off and the ignition was cut. The van's side doors opened slowly while five men jumped out. All of them were fully dressed in black.

Keys jingling against his waist, the leader quickly picked the front door lock. They all entered the house closing the door behind them. Patiently, the trespassers searched the rooms, the attic, and closets for any connection to the sinkhole mystery. They found the staircase to the basement. Hurriedly, they went down the steps with their head flashlights guiding the way. They quickly searched the laboratory. One of the agents found notes and drawings of the gizmos that Declan had carelessly left on a wooden table. "Now we have something. Let's move out."

All five men tidied up the house and then quietly drove off without any witnesses to their home invasion. The boss picked up his radio transmitter and whispered to someone on the receiving end, "It's time to capture them; green light for Operation Gaul." He smirked at the driver next to him as they drove to their underground scientific lab not far from the San Francisco airport.

✦

After a long thirteen-hour flight, the family's jet plane landed safely in Paris' Charles de Gaulle Airport. It was cold in December, colder than the winters California offered. Feeling excited, the family visited sites such as the Notre Dame Cathedral, The Royal Palace, The Louvre Museum, and rode the metro everywhere. The twins were impressed with the intricate underground network of train stops, tunnels, and malls that were interwoven.

Mr. and Mrs. Salk had decided to save the Eiffel Tower for their last tourist stop in France and had booked their elevator tickets online for the afternoon on the fourth day. On that day, they rode over on line number six from the Place d'Italie near their hotel. They got off the metro at the elevated station Bir-Hakeim and weaved their way around the crowds, walking briskly toward the Eiffel Tower. The city was bustling with speedy traffic and pedestrians exhaling their steamy breaths. Upon arriving at the famous construction, they went up in the elevators to the highest of the three balconies.

"What a terrific view!" Dalya was elated.

"Wow!" whispered Declan to himself.

"What do you think about the view?" asked Mrs. Salk.

"Paris is beautiful. What a fantastic-looking old city it is, Mom," Dalya exclaimed.

After about a half hour of gazing at the city from the deck's perimeter, Mom and Dad decided to visit the post office and the exhibition on the largest balcony.

"Declan, Dalya, we are taking the lifts down to the first level. Do you want anything?"

"No thanks, Mom," both twins answered.

"Okay, you can stay up here if you want. How about we meet at the first balcony in front of the post office in an hour? We'll see you a bit later," replied Dad.

The twins felt excited to be in Europe with all of its sensational sights, smells, and sounds. They decided to take the lift down to the middle balcony. Feeling mesmerized by the scenic view from the deck, the siblings walked around and explored every centimeter of the Tower's amazing structure. They separated, each walking off in the opposite direction, anxious to see more. After a few minutes, an elevator carried up some more tourists to the middle deck.

The last person out of the elevator was a thin, young woman dressed in dark clothing. She wore a thick ski jacket with a hood draped over her head. Under the hood, the woman wore a warm tourist beanie hat with the words "Power of the Tower" etched in yellow on an Eiffel Tower patch. It wasn't a typical tourist hat. Searching desperately, quickly breathing in the cold air, she had to reach the twins before the *others* did. The woman was desperate to talk with the twins, to warn them of the dangers to come.

Dalya was now somberly sitting on a bench looking around the deck. She began to have doubts about finding the secret messenger she and Declan were to meet. Then, the young woman slowly approached the twin in order to not startle her.

"Dalya?" the woman gently addressed the girl.

"Huh?" Dalya responded, feeling both surprised and uneasy. "Yes, that is my name. Who are you?"

"I'm the person who sent you the message. I'm the one who asked you to meet me here."

The twin stood up quietly and remained in a fixed position, uncertain if she should run or stay with this stranger. Before this moment, Dalya was eager to find the person who wrote her the coded message. Now she wasn't so sure. Dalya felt scared and wanted this whole situation to go away and to return to her peaceful, happy life before the sinkhole discovery. Unfortunately, her wish would not be fulfilled. Should she run and find Declan to warn him?

"You figured out the puzzle, nice work. I knew you could do it," the woman said breaking a smile. "Dalya, you must listen to me very carefully. What I'm going to tell you is very important, important to you and to the world. I know about your and Declan's secret. We have been tracking and investigating you for the past two months. We know you have the power to become invisible."

Dalya held her breath and hesitated to speak about her valuable secret to this friendly yet mysterious stranger.

The woman sensed Dalya's nervousness. "I can prove that I'm your friend who wants to help by asking you some simple questions. Answer with a nod. You received a coded message to meet someone here. The coded words are *Time flies with jet wings*, *Gustav's tall construction*, and *Enter second stage*. Is this correct?"

Dalya, feeling suspicious, held the woman's gaze, while both stood silently staring at each other.

"Who else would know this other than you, your brother, and me? Think about it," the woman insisted. "You can trust me. I'm here to help you." She held her right hand wide open at her own chest. The woman needed to win Dalya's trust in order to help her.

The twin slowly drew in her breath and hesitantly whispered a cautious "Yes." She began to feel comfortable with this woman. Dalya realized she is in this situation, full on, with no way to return to her previous life. Also, if she wanted to learn more about her invisible powers, she had better cooperate with this stranger who may have some helpful information.

The woman slowly exhaled with relief, leaving a steamy cloud in the cold air. The temperature had dropped considerably, and the sky turned gray. An hour had passed since they had arrived at the Eiffel Tower. A light snowfall began to claim the sky.

"What I'm about to tell you is highly confidential. You must promise not to tell anyone but Declan, all right?"

"I promise."

"Very well then, my name is Kate, and I work for a specialized scientific military unit called SOUP. It stands for *Scientists Of Undercover Projects*. We are specially trained agents who trek around the world to investigate unusual activities and phenomena. As I mentioned before, we know you can become invisible. We still don't understand how or why you came upon this ability. We've investigated the sinkhole you and Declan were at nearly two months ago and have become aware that there is some kind of connection between that hole and your invisible powers. Several holes have been discovered around the United States, mostly in isolated places."

"I understand."

"We know for certain that Argentina, Mexico, New Zealand, Japan, and Peru have them as well. Quite possibly more people have developed the anomalies you have."

"You mean people from these countries became invisible from those sinkholes like my brother and I?"

"It's possible; however, we don't know enough yet as these governments aren't cooperating with us. It's hard for us to get to the sinkholes to analyze them or to find the people who may have discovered them by accident. Like you and your brother, these people wouldn't want to be found. Until now, all we know is that you and Declan are the only living proof or evidence of these invisible powers. Can I ask you some questions?"

"Yes. Go ahead."

"To begin with, how do you turn invisible?"

"I don't know. I guess it just happens randomly," Dalya lied as she wasn't ready to reveal their invention.

"What happens to you when you become invisible? How do you feel? Can you and Declan see each other when you are invisible? Can—"

"Wait! You are going too fast. How am I going to answer your questions if I'm not allowed any time?"

Dalya asked rhetorically.

"Oh, I'm so sorry. It's just incredible to meet someone like you. In my field of work, one waits a long time to find someone with your powers."

"Look, before I answer your questions, tell me why my brother and I are in danger." Dalya's eyes squinted and locked on Kate's.

The SOUP agent carefully looked around. When she was satisfied that no one was listening close by, she continued.

"You see, SOUP has begun to separate itself from the military and is now pursuing its own goals. It wants to control your powers, to learn about them, and to use invisibility to rule the world."

"But aren't you one of them?"

"Yes and no. I also work for another group that wants to prevent SOUP to fulfill their agenda, therefore we don't want SOUP to capture you and use your powers. I have penetrated SOUP and am working undercover. We don't know yet everything about who really controls SOUP, but they are determined experts, who will not rest until they have control of your powers. Do you see now why you are in grave danger, Dalya?"

Dalya felt dizzy upon hearing Kate's news. "Who's that other group you're working for?"

"I am not yet ready to say. You just have to trust me. At this point, you'll be safer not knowing."

While Dalya and the woman were talking, Declan was busy studying the rivets and bolts joining the crisscrossing metallic patterns that banded together the Eiffel Tower's body. Just then, off in the distant sky behind him, he heard rotor sounds chopping through the air. He immediately went to the balcony's rail and placed his bare hands on the frosty, metal rim of the safety fence. Declan squinted toward the eastern horizon and soon realized that three black Apache-style attack helicopters flew parallel to the Tower's balcony. Declan had an uneasy feeling about those machines. Throughout his childhood, his intuition had always kept him out of trouble. Suddenly, the machines steered ninety-degrees, flying directly at him.

The helicopters became louder as they steadily closed in on the Tower. He had to find his sister. While scurrying around the balcony, he saw Dalya and a woman engaged in deep conversation. The two figures stood stiffly about twenty meters away from him. Declan immediately commanded his gizmo and within a flash turned invisible as he approached them.

"Here!" Kate stretched out her hand to give a piece of paper to Dalya. "This is the next coded message for you to decipher. Please follow whatever it asks of you. I'm told the instructions are important to help you learn more about your powers."

Just then, Declan shouted, "Dalya, they're coming. Let's get out of here."

Kate and Dalya both sprang into action. Kate cried out, "I mustn't be caught. Remember, follow the coded instructions!"

As the double agent said these words, Dalya pressed

her gizmo button and dematerialized right in front of Kate, but the agent didn't notice as she was preparing to climb over the safety fence to jump off the balcony. The well-trained SOUP woman leaped over into the gray, cold sky.

"Kaaaaaate!" Dalya thought Kate had plummeted to her death, but the agent had opened a mini parachute. The astonished twin watched Kate as she landed safely on the ground below at an angle that allowed her to run as soon as her feet touched the ground. The woman dashed off through the Champ de Mars field as she quickly unfastened her parachute. She ran for a hundred yards to a black speed motorcycle. Kate started it up with one downward push of her right foot and roared off into the evening.

"C'mon sis." The invisible twins ran toward the lift. Declan glanced behind his shoulder and noticed one of the black-clothed men leaning out of the lead helicopter. He held a fist-sized radar gun of some kind and it was aimed right at him and his sister. A red faint transparent light emanated from its nozzle. "What's that?" he wondered. The twins' instincts warned them to stay out of its path. The helicopters' noises were deafening as they hovered just several meters away from the balcony. The twins ran to the south elevator. "We need to stay out of the way of those men and that radar device," Declan instructed.

"Let's hide inside and wait for the next tourist group to come up, then we'll invisibly enter the elevator to go down," Dalya suggested. They ran inside to the snack bar.

Looking through the glass windows, the twins could see two men swing onto the balcony from cables connected to one of the helicopters. One of them talked into his wrist radio, pointing a finger toward the lift. In the meantime, more agents were racing up the steps in each of the Tower's legs. The agents wore knitted black head covers with only the eyes exposed. In shock, tourists just stepped away from the men. For the next minute, the twins scuttled around indoors and ducked behind whatever objects they could find that would provide valuable cover from the secret agents and their threatening ray guns.

The lift came. A crowd of anxious tourists had already formed in front of the entrance in a rush to get off the deck. The new arrivals tried to file out of the elevator while the fleeing tourists piled in. Taking advantage of the chaos, the twins stood up from behind an empty serving counter next to the kitchen and sped like gazelles into the lift. The doors closed, and the elevator conductor pressed a button to allow the elevator to start its slow descent to the first balcony.

"Look at what's happening, Declan!" Dalya whispered. The twins looked out of the elevator's windows. "They're coming for us." Several meters above the elevator, two stealthy men repelled slowly down the slanted elevator shaft.

Declan appeared surprisingly calm. "They will somehow try to apprehend us as soon as the lift's doors open at the next stop. We must escape without them noticing."

Startled, a teenage American tourist girl looked over wondering where the whispers were coming from. The twins fell silent. As she didn't hear anything more, the girl became disinterested and turned her head away from them.

Hearts thumped, breaths quickened as the twins waited for the lift to inch its way down, centimeter by centimeter.

The first balcony's square area was significantly larger than the other two. The elevator slowed to a stop. The doors slid open. Two goggled hunters were waiting in front of them. One agent had a ray gun, the other a round black thumper gun, set on stun.

"Never seen that before," Declan pondered to himself. Panic and confusion increased within the lift. The passengers noticed the hostile men and cried for help. The men loudly barked something to the passengers. Chaotically, the people rushed out. Suddenly, a ray beam shined upon and exposed the twins. They appeared in the agents' goggles as pink translucent figures crouched in the far corners of the lift. After a split second, Declan yelled "Now!"

They sprang forward from their positions. In a flash, they rushed by the two agents, who fumbled around looking for them while unsuccessfully pointing their ray guns everywhere. The two men lost their invisible prey and radioed for help.

Two helicopters had already landed on the plaza. Several men blocked the elevators' ground entrances. By this time, a medium-sized crowd of people had gathered around to watch the action. The third machine slowly circled around the balcony, searching for any signs of the twins' presence. Another beam, this time from the helicopter, shined its red band of energy onto the platform looking for the two runners.

"Ready, set, jump!" Dalya shouted.

The fleeing twins leaped off the balcony opposite from where the helicopter's current position was. When the two siblings had rushed out of the elevator, they had snatched the two agents' repelling cables from the side of their belts. Each cable was in a small square container, like a tape measure. They repelled quickly yet clumsily to the ground. Declan detached his cable container from his belt and let it go. It immediately went flying back up to the balcony where the hook was attached to the rail. The cable banged into the hook with a loud *Clang*. A second after, Dalya's cable rig did the same.

The two now-desperate agents heard this and without hesitation ran toward the sounds. They reached the cables, stared down at their belts, and realized what had transpired. By now, more men with thumper guns had arrived on the balcony. The first agent radioed and yelled, "They are on the ground. Search the plaza!" About a dozen more agents immediately sprang to action, executing a fanned perimeter sweep of the plaza and fields. They looked around, barking orders at each other.

The man with the jingling keys was disappointed. He contemplated the situation, lifted his hand radio to his mouth, and in a controlled, commanding voice ordered, "All units, let's get to work on finding those kids, right now! Whoever finds them first will be promoted."

✦

Some minutes later, Declan and Dalya snuck into a closed park by climbing its tall wrought iron gates. They found a private place among some thickets and sat on an old, dirty cement bench. It was now dusk and much colder. The Parisian street lamps flickered on.

"Who was that woman you were talking with, Dalya?"

"Her name is Kate. She's the one who sent us the message that led us to the Eiffel Tower. She works undercover in an organization called SOUP which stands for *Scientists Of Undercover Projects*. The men who chased us must be part of it. They want to capture us and use our powers to rule the world."

"It sounds like a seriously dangerous organization."

"Yes, it does. Kate gave me another message. It'll tell us what we should do next."

Reaching into her pocket with trembling hands, she pulled out the small slip of paper Kate had given her. Dalya was nervous and scared, yet excited by all of the action that had happened in the last several minutes. For her, time was moving at rocket speed.

"Let's have a look at it. Well, another riddle to figure out. It's a poem, Dalya."

They huddled together.

"It's getting dark. Read it quickly, Declan."

"All right, here we go." He read the entire poem two

times while Dalya remained thoughtfully silent.

Amazing and oh so complex greens
Pathways of the twelve concentric rings
High hedges acceding
The tower waits for what the next nightfall brings
Napoleon defeated by tricky orienteering

"I think I know what this message is communicating, Dalya. It's referring to a location, perhaps a meeting place. Look at the fourth line. It means tomorrow night we are to meet someone at a tower of some kind when the sky becomes dark. The first line means that the place we'll meet at is some kind of garden, or park, or something. The third line obviously means this place has high hedges and plants of some sort. I still haven't figured out the second and last lines."

"The second line might refer to maze designs. We are to meet someone at a maze, a turf maze, which is also known as a plant maze."

"You're right, sis. It seems to refer to a maze pattern developed centuries ago. The concentric rings mean that the garden we need to find has overlapping circular paths in it. The tower mentioned in line four must be the meeting place within or near the maze."

Dalya inquired, "Do you think the labyrinth will be difficult to get through to reach the tower?"

"First of all, we are not looking for a labyrinth. There is a difference between a labyrinth and a maze. Historically, labyrinths were made with only one way to get in and out. Hence, there is only one path or solution to the labyrinth. No dead ends and false ways to trick you. A maze has more than one way to get in and out of it and has false ways and dead ends. Mazes are much more complicated."

"How do we know we are looking for a maze and not a labyrinth?"

"Well, read the first word of this riddle. *Amazing* is the first word. Its letters *m*, *a*, *z* spell most of the word *maze*. My guess is the letters reveal that we are looking for a maze."

Dalya summarized as she took in a long breath, "So, what we know is that we are looking for a turf maze. The maze has a tower somewhere in it. And, the maze has a circular shape of some kind."

"Yes, Dalya. And according to line four, we are to be at the tower around nightfall to meet someone who will give us more information about why we are in danger."

"For what purpose were mazes created for?"

"Well, Dalya, throughout history, since the Egyptians until the Middle Ages, kings and nobles created mazes to protect themselves from enemy attacks on their homes. During the Middle Ages, mazes would slow enemies down to give time for a castle's residents to hide underground or escape through another route. A lot of times they were built as ditches and filled with water, acting as protective moats. Natural plant mazes and stone mazes were built all over the world. The ancient Egyptians built mazes into pyramids to hide their Pharaohs' corpses and the treasures buried within from temple robbers. Now, what we need to figure out is where this turf maze is. The last line should hold the clue."

The siblings sat on the bench for a while, both crouching over the mysterious message. After about five minutes of pondering the riddle, Declan propped up suddenly. "I think I know what the last line is telling us. Do you know who Napoleon was, Dalya?"

"A French general."

"Correct, Napoleon was a famous French general, a skillful general who knew how to lead armies to win big battles. After the French Revolution, he helped France to become a stable country. With his armies, the general conquered most of the Western World. In 1804, he made himself emperor when he was only thirty-five years old. His empire stretched from Spain to Egypt. I found a book about Napoleon's life in our local library. One of the chapters described how he had visited a garden while traveling through Italy. He went into the maze garden and couldn't find his way out. His entourage went into the garden to retrieve him. Isn't that incredible? A superb military general, who had conquered most of the West at the time, got lost in a garden? The maze must be complicated if Napoleon was duped."

"Where in Italy is this maze?"

"The maze is in the town of Villa Pisani. It's near Venice," Declan said with certainty.

"I'm calling Mom and Dad to let them know where we are." Dalya quickly chatted with Mom on her cell phone. She finished her conversation and pocketed her gadget. "So, they were upset, but I told them we are fine. They are on their way down to meet us at the metro station's entrance we used before."

"Dalya, don't you think it is strange that the next clue leads us to Italy when our plan is to already fly to Venice tomorrow morning?"

"Kate told me she tracked us down. The organization must know all about the internet bookings Dad had made for our trip. How else would they know about our plans and when we would be on the Eiffel Tower? The online elevator tickets are only valid for a certain time."

"You're right, but what about the hotel?" Declan exclaimed, "They must be waiting for us there."

"I think we are safe. Remember that we couldn't stay at the first hotel because of an overbooking and Dad insisted on finding a quaint little hotel on his own?"

"Yes, I do. We were so annoyed, but at the end, it's a blessing in disguise."

Declan suggested, "We could convince Mom and Dad to visit the turf maze since Villa Pisani is only about twenty miles from Venice. We could shoot over there on a bus or taxi. I bet our parents would go for that." It was completely dark now. The twins still heard the helicopters in the distance going about their relentless search.

"Declan, don't you think we should tell Mom and Dad about our powers? I mean, it isn't fair to keep all of this hidden from them. After all, they trust us fully and are always open with us about everything."

"Yes. Mom and Dad deserve to know. After all of

the action today, maybe they already have a hunch."

"I don't think so, Declan. We were invisible during the whole thing so they couldn't have seen us being chased around."

Declan added, "But let's get more information at this next location so we can tell them what is really going on. Once we have more facts, we'll ask for their help."

They stood up from the bench and walked toward the metro station. The twins remained invisible to protect themselves from any SOUP agents or French police who might also be searching for them. As they neared the metro's entrance, they ducked into an empty alley and whispered to their gizmos. The two figures rematerialized. Tired and hungry, they jogged the remaining distance to the station and met their worried parents. The twins conjured up a story on why they were late. Although concerned, Mr. and Mrs. Salk seemed somewhat satisfied with the story.

Dinner consisted of Vietnamese food in the Asian quarter behind their hotel. During the warm, friendly dinner conversation, the parents agreed it was a good idea to travel to the maze. Mr. and Mrs. Salk were pleased the children were so interested in discovering Europe and had travel ideas of their own.

Who would the twins meet at the mysterious tower and what adventures await them?

6 Project Rainbow ✦

Vroom! A motor scooter roared past the twins. "Watch out, Dalya!"

The startled twin quickly sidestepped out of the scooter's path just as it whined by, missing her by a few centimeters.

"Whew, that was close."

Just then, an English-speaking tourist bumped into the twins. Declan fell down backwards while a large man stepped back and caught his balance.

"Hey, what did I bump into?" asked the man. He was taking photos with his wife.

"I don't know, honey. There's nothing here," the wife said curiously. She was waving her hands in midair, feeling for something located on the sidewalk.

"Let's go, dear." The tourists went on their way, leaving behind the nervous invisible twins.

"First, the scooter nearly slammed us and now this incident. Maybe we should reappear again," Declan suggested.

"No, Declan. The more we remain invisible, the safer we are. Maybe those SOUP goons followed us here and are spying on us as we speak. Or, they want to try to catch us again."

"You're right. Let's sightsee and enjoy Venice while we're invisible. We just have to be careful. It's as crowded as an ant colony around here."

The twins visited all of the wonderful sights Venice had to offer. Mr. and Mrs. Salk decided to sleep in at the hotel and graciously allowed the siblings two hours alone to discover the watery city's architectural gifts. Later, the family met in the city's center. Touring the canals on the famous drifting Venetian boats, the travelers were captivated by the enriching colors, sounds, and odors, all of which tantalized their senses.

Invisibility wasn't an option while the twins traveled with their parents. Although invisibility had its risks, being visible made the siblings feel more vulnerable. Constantly deciding when and where to be visible or invisible increasingly became an emotional strain for them.

Late afternoon was now approaching.

"Mom, Dad? Could we go see that maze now?" Dalya begged.

"Sure we can," said Dad. "Let's go catch the last tourist bus the information center told us about."

The family walked briskly to avoid being late. They boarded the half empty bus and sat on some rickety wooden seats. Twenty minutes later, the family hopped out of the idling bus which stopped at a quaint little village named Stra next to Villa Pisani. They strolled through Stra toward Pisani. The maze the family was going to tackle was created sometime in the early eighteenth century. It was once considered the world's most complicated maze.

By now, the sun was minutes away from kissing the horizon which generously gave the sky an array of colors. There were only a few other tourists at the site. The Salks took their time wandering through the concentric circular layers the maze slowly unfolded before them. Dusk would arrive soon. Both feeling impatient, the twins stopped and turned to their parents.

"Mom, Dad, could Dalya and I tackle this maze alone? We want to reach that tower at the center."

Mr. Salk replied, "Sure, how about we meet you in forty-five minutes at the entrance?"

"Excellent! We'll see you then," Dalya confirmed. Feeling relieved, the twins trailed off through one of the winding paths.

"Declan, I'm still feeling bothered that we haven't told Mom and Dad about us."

"Yeah, I know. But it's like we've discussed before. It's no use getting them involved in any kind of danger until we know what's really going on. Hopefully, after we meet this mysterious person, we'll know more, and then we could explain everything to Mom and Dad. Let's decide what to do after tonight." Despite his words, Declan also tried to convince himself they were doing the right thing.

The twins shuffled through the complicated winding paths. They were eager to get to the tower.

"Should we separate?" asked Dalya. "What if we take too much time to find the right path? The person might not wait so long."

"You're right. Let's separate and meet at the tower's entrance. But let's become invisible just in case this is a trap of some kind."

"Good idea. I'll see you at the tower. Be safe."

"You do the same."

On their commands, their bodies dematerialized as they departed in opposite directions. After fifteen frustrating minutes, the anticipation of reaching the tower turned to near agony for both. Many different times each would wander forward, stop, retrace the steps, and then move onward to a new pathway. Finally, the twins reached the structure nearly at the same moment. They stood next to each other and silently agreed with a head nod to remain completely quiet. Declan signaled with his hand at Dalya to examine the first floor while he'll cover the upper levels. Dalya entered the small dark room. She heard Declan's footsteps fading as he wound his way up the six-meter tower. Descending down the steps, Declan shrugged his shoulders.

"All right, no one here either," Dalya sighed breaking the silence.

"I think it's safe to become visible again," Declan suggested.

"Yes. Let's do it."

They rematerialized and wondered what to do next when they heard someone's voice.

"*Pssst, Pssst!*"

Instinctually, they quickly ducked down as if shielding themselves from a swarm of bees.

"Over here. Behind the tower opposite the entrance," the voice urgently whispered.

Declan and Dalya looked at each other with puzzled expressions, then stepped out of the tower and followed the voice. An elderly woman sat quietly on a green wooden bench just around a bend leading away from the tower.

"Who are you?" Dalya asked.

"Just address me as Ms. Blodgett," the woman dictated in a stern voice. "Kate informed me that you may show up. Well done on solving the riddles and finding your way through the maze. You are clever children, I must say."

Ms. Blodgett had an educated English accent. She wore a black headscarf and a long black coat which covered her black slacks. In one hand, she held a cane with a brass handle of a lion's head. One leg was crossed over the other. Based on her tone, she seemed to have an intolerant disposition toward teenagers.

"I have heard you ran into a bit of trouble in Paris. Well, now you have a glimpse of the precarious circumstances you are in. These people will not rest until they catch you because they want to study and obtain your powers for their own use."

"Yes, we know. Kate already told me in Paris."

Dalya felt impatient and wanted to get information from this mysterious woman about her and Declan's powers. Standing in the maze in front of Ms. Blodgett, Dalya began to feel trapped. A claustrophobic sensation began to sweep over her. She and Declan were easy targets here.

"What I am about to tell you cannot—*must not*—be shared with anyone. It is imperative that the knowledge you gain here today remains only with you. Can you promise me? Humanity depends on your secrecy."

The twins felt startled by Ms. Blodgett's urgent tone and her insistence on making this promise. After a slight hesitation, they harmoniously responded, "We promise."

Both parties now became interlocked by their curiosity for one another. For a short duration, Ms. Blodgett and the twins remained silent as they assessed the situation unfolding before them. The woman wondered if she could trust these two young, inexperienced teens with the important secrets she would impart upon them. The twins both wondered whether to stay here with this strange black-clad woman or run away. Their curiosity won over as they chose to stay.

Ms. Blodgett began. "All right then. A long time ago, an experiment was conducted in the year 1943, during the month of October. A strange thing happened—"

"What happened?" Dalya asked.

"No questions, please," the woman responded impatiently. "We do not have time for questions. Just listen to what is being said. The US Navy had been working on a top-secret science experiment involving invisibility. It was known as *The Philadelphia Experiment* or *Project Rainbow* by some. Rendering objects invisible was of special interest to the American navy. Your military people believed this would give them an advantage over the enemy during World War Two."

"Wow! It's hard to believe people were thinking about invisibility way back then."

The woman remained silent, eyeballing Declan with disapproval for interrupting. When Declan stopped smiling and settled his emotions, the elegant woman continued without losing her rhythm.

"The US Navy believed that it could achieve a quick victory over the Axis powers if it could fight with invisible ships, airplanes, tanks, and soldiers. On October 28, 1943, the USS *Eldridge* was selected for this experiment. Large generators were placed all over its decks. These machines would be switched on and then give out an electromagnetic charge all around the ship, which would bend the light around the vessel. Once light is bent, scientists thought, the object would become invisible. The ship and the men onboard actually did vanish for a few minutes. Before the *Eldridge* disappeared, witnesses reported that a greenish, glowing fog had surrounded the ship until the vessel had truly become invisible!"

Declan and Dalya's stomachs churned with shock and excitement. Both twins swallowed hard. They stared at Ms. Blodgett in anticipation for more information.

She continued, "The ship was successfully cloaked, but there were unexpected side effects with the experiment."

"What kinds of side effects?" Declan interrupted again.

Ms. Blodgett began to feel more comfortable with the twins. "Well, the ship reappeared in the exact location where it had vanished, at Philadelphia's naval shipyard in Pennsylvania. However, during its disappearance, the ship had been sighted at a different location. Suddenly, the vessel sat in the water at another port in Norfolk, Virginia over two hundred miles away. Witnesses, men aboard another military ship called the USS *Andrew Furuseth*, described the ship resting in the water next to them for a short period of time before it vanished from Norfolk amidst a green foggy haze. Shortly thereafter, the *Eldridge* reappeared again in the Philadelphia naval yard. The *Eldridge* had been accidentally teleported to another place. Now, any military that could render objects invisible and teleport them would be the most powerful force on the Earth."

The woman's face looked weary and expressed deep concern.

"What does the USS *Eldridge* have to do with us?"

Ms. Blodgett stared at Declan for several seconds, feeling frustrated that he didn't understand the obvious.

"Don't you see, my dear? The navy and probably others are still experimenting to perfect the invisibility problem. Finally, the problem could be solved if they had other examples, like you, to help complete their work. You two are the answer to their dreams."

Anxiously, Dalya asked, "What do you mean 'to perfect'? Did something happen to the *Eldridge* ship?"

"Very peculiar things occurred. It is said that when the ship reappeared, strange events had taken place. The experimenters saw that some of the sailors' bodies were literally melted into the ship's metal. One sailor's hand was sort of glued to the ship's deck. Another sailor was teleported to the deck below from the deck above where he had stood at the beginning of the ship's disappearance. Some of the men onboard reported feeling sick and nauseated. In the months following the experiment, other sailors were known to go insane."

Pausing for a moment, Ms. Blodgett allowed the twins to absorb and digest these strange and disturbing events. The siblings stared at each other before snapping out of their speechless state of mind.

"Well, nothing of that sort has happened to us, Ms. Blodgett. So far, Dalya and I couldn't be healthier, right?" Declan glanced over to his sister, looking for a reassuring answer.

"That's definitely correct."

The woman smiled. "Well, I am very happy to hear that fate has worked out better for you than for those poor sailors from long ago. You must listen to me now. We are almost finished here. You have realized from your recent experiences that there is a secret group that wants to capture you."

"What about you, Ms. Blodgett? Are you one of those people who want to capture us? Is this meeting just a trap?" Dalya frowned.

"Oh no, dear, if I had wanted to capture you, I would have done so back in Paris or even before. My role here is to help Kate and others to make you aware of what you are involved in and to keep you from being harmed."

"So who else wants to help us?"

"There is no time to answer more questions now, young lady. You will find out soon enough. Here, take this."

The woman thrust out her gloved hand and uncurled her fingers to reveal a gold sprocket container. Dalya stretched out her arms and carefully let the object fall into her cupped hands.

"What is this?" the twins asked in unison.

"This, my young adventurers, is a cryptex. If you decipher the code from this machine, you will be able to unlock it and access an important scrolled message inside. The cryptogram will lead you to another location where you will find more information to help you understand what to do next. With the knowledge you will acquire, you can learn more about your incredible gifts and the wicked people who are trying to capture you. That is all, children."

"Ms. Blodgett, thank you for all of your help," Declan said pleasantly.

"Before we separate, you must know one other important thing. If you try to force or break your way into the cryptex, the chemical solution inside will soak and destroy the paper and the message it contains. Figure out the password, and the cryptex will unlock itself. Here is your clue—"

"Wait! Why don't you just tell us more about all of this? Or, why not just tell us where to go next?"

Before the woman could answer, Dalya suddenly jumped in and answered, "Since Ms. Blodgett has limited information to pass on, we won't be able to reveal too many secrets if we are caught by SOUP or any other interested parties. Also, for security reasons, she won't even know where we're supposed to go next. Am I right, Ms. Blodgett?"

The woman smiled in admiration. "Yes, you are, clever girl. Are you ready for the clue?"

Enthralled, the twins answered with a quiet nod of their heads, not wanting to miss any instructions Ms. Blodgett would give them.

"Of Pisa he came, Zero is his game."

Ms. Blodgett paused and then slowly added, "There is your clue. Goodbye to you and good luck."

Without a handshake or another word, Ms. Blodgett abruptly rose to her feet and briskly walked away from the twins, displaying a cold countenance. She rounded a path's green hedges and quietly disappeared. The mysterious woman left their lives as suddenly as she had entered them. Declan and Dalya looked at each other inquisitively, intrigued by Ms. Blodgett and her elusive behavior.

The twins heard their parents approaching them, footsteps thudding heavily on the cement path. Mom and Dad found the way to the tower and greeted their children with a hug. Dalya had already pocketed the cryptex, hiding it from view.

Dad explained, "Hi! We thought we heard your voices."

Feeling a bit exhausted from being out all day in the cold temperatures, the family decided to walk slowly back to the station and boarded the bus. After a while, the bus roared to life and sputtered out its black exhaust smoke as it drove away from the turf maze. Ms. Blodgett followed it with a contemplative gaze.

She whispered to herself, "Good luck, young adventurers, and be careful."

Dusk had overtaken the sky, and the stars began their twilight dances.

7 Liber Abaci ✦

"Look, the cryptic lock consists of ten separate spirals. Each spiral contains all of the letters of our alphabet." Dalya examined the container while sitting on her bed.

"Yes, that means there must be an endless number of possible combinations," Declan added, feeling a bit unnerved. "Dalya, grab that pencil and paper pad over there. I'm curious how many combinations there are."

After a delicious pizza dinner at a local restaurant the twins went to their bedroom in a quiet little inn. Two separate rooms had been rented for the night. Their room stood directly across from their parents' room. The corridor had an old wooden floor and walls covered with tapestries, which smelled of many visitors from the past. With its original iron chandeliers, artwork, and other objects from its inception, the five-hundred-year-old hotel still kept its rustic charm.

The two decoders worked into the late evening to figure out the password.

"Let's see. The number of combinations will be twenty-six times ten, which gives…260 combinations." Declan paused. "Wait a minute. That's not the correct math." He caught his mathematical mistake.

"No, it isn't. That number is too low, Declan. Each dial has twenty-six letters. There are ten dials. Ten dials multiplied by twenty-six letters only give you the total number of letters on the cryptex, not the total number of combinations all ten dials can form."

Dalya held the cryptex up and pointed to each dial column as she thoroughly explained how to calculate the extraordinarily large number of possible letter combinations the machine can produce.

Declan reiterated, "You're correct. We'll have to multiply twenty-six by itself ten times over." He then scribbled down the math problem: *26 x 26 x 26 x 26 x 26 x 26 x 26 x 26 x 26 x 26=?*

"Oh my goodness, the answer is in the millions! Twenty-six to the power of ten is a huge number." Declan felt amazed and frustrated at the same time. "How are we going to crack this code?"

Patiently, Dalya responded, "Let's go through the clues we have, step by step. The first part of Ms. Blodgett's statement is *Of Pisa he came*. Pisa is a city here in Italy with the famous Leaning Tower. The word *he* must refer to a male. Maybe the clue is about a man or a boy from Pisa."

"Right! The second part of the sentence *Zero is his game* probably means he has something to do with mathematics."

"All right, now we may be getting somewhere. The next question is, which mathematicians come from Pisa?" Dalya inquired.

"We could ask Dad to lend us his phone. He's got internet access. We could tell him we'd like to do some research on the maze." Declan jumped up, left the room, and came back a minute later with the phone in his hand and a smile on his face. "I knew Dad would give us his phone."

"Good. Let's investigate."

After punching in the key words *mathematician*, *Italy*, *Pisa* and *Zero*, the different search results repeatedly displayed the name of a certain mathematician called *Leonardo Pisano Bigollo*, appearing also on the screen as *Leonardo Bonacci* or *Fibonacci*.

"Fibonacci! That must be the letter combination. Let's try it," suggested Dalya.

She quickly tweaked the dials to spell out the name *Fibonacci*. When she reached the tenth and last letter, the flustered girl looked up in disappointment. "We are one letter short, Declan. The name only has nine letters. We need ten."

"All right, we made a careless error, so let's move on and learn about him." Declan read aloud the following, "Leonardo of Pisa, or Fibonacci, lived from AD 1180 to 1250 and was a mathematician and scholar. He was born to a wealthy Italian merchant who traded in northern Africa. Leonardo traveled with his father to Africa, and it was there that he learned about Hindu-Arabic numerals. Fibonacci thought the Arabic numeral system with the digit *zero* was much easier to use compared to the Roman numeral system already in place in Europe."

"Keep reading. There must be more clues," Dalya

insisted impatiently.

"However, the conceptual mathematic symbol *0* first came to Europe from India. In AD 830, an Indian man named Al-Khwarizmi explained how the zero worked in Indian numerals, but his writings were not translated for another four hundred years. Zero continued to puzzle mathematicians. Was zero a number or a digit? Did it mean nothing or did it have some mathematical value? If zero meant nothing, then why did the Indians go through the trouble of explaining its use a long time ago?"

"That's a good question," Dalya interjected.

"Leonardo of Pisa wrote a book titled *Liber Abaci*. Translated, the title is *The Book of Calculation*, which is one of the first books in the West to describe Arabic numerals. Fibonacci said that zero can be used as a placeholder to separate columns or figures. It can also represent a position on a scale. In temperature scales, zero represents a true value. Zero means something. It does not mean 'no temperature'. Leonardo solved the puzzle of zero. Ever since zero was accepted as a numerical value, Arabic numerals and algebra replaced the Roman numeral system in Europe."

Both twins remained silent for a few minutes, sitting on the bed while staring at the small screen. Dalya spoke first. "This guy Fibonacci was amazing. It's incredible how algebra made its way from India to Europe and then to the rest of the world!"

"Dalya, let's go through the article again and find our password."

As soon as Declan finished his statement, Dalya

whispered in controlled excitement, "*Liber Abaci.*" She repeated the two words to herself. "The book title—it has ten letters. Could it be that easy? Out of millions of combinations of letters, is this it?"

Staring at all ten fingers in disbelief, Declan said each letter slowly aloud, "L-i-b-e-r-a-b-a-c-i."

Dalya moved the dials with her right thumb to spell out the two words. The suspense was excruciating. Dalya meticulously turned each column as if each letter was a fragile piece of crystal. She was careful not to force the machine out of fear that she might break it and never uncover its secrets. Sweat began to pour from each twin's temples. The fifth dial column clicked in, then the sixth, then the seventh. Dalya's fingers began to tremble slightly in nervous anticipation. "Will this work?" she contemplated.

Click, sounded the eighth letter as it set in its rightful place. *Click*, went the ninth letter to its designated place. Dalya looked up slowly toward her brother. She paused to regain composure. Declan had his palms pressed together tightly and then placed them softly on his nose. He silently nodded. Dalya began to turn the tenth and final dial. Slowly from *x* she turned it to *y* and then began at *a*, maneuvering her fingers on the sprocket and guiding the letters slowly to reach *i*.

Click! The cryptex automatically unlocked and loosened in Dalya's sweaty grip. She slid the machine apart, separating its two main pieces to reveal a secret compartment. Declan took the inner chamber out and removed a small scroll. He slowly unrolled it, feeling excited about what the paper would reveal. The old brown sheet spit out a crackling sound.

"Be careful, Declan," Dalya told him forcefully, "It looks very old."

What they saw was completely unexpected! A calligraphic written series of the numbers 3 5 18 14 was followed by the words *NIHIL RESPONSUM*.

"What is *NIHIL RESPONSUM?* What do those numbers mean, Dalya?"

"Oh my, I think I might know. In fifth grade, our math teacher, Mrs. Mayer, taught us about the Fibonacci sequence where one number is always the sum of the previous two numbers. Look at the first two numbers. This sequence starts at number three which is the sum of one and two, then five is the sum of two and three, then 18 is the sum of— no, wait. The pattern breaks apart here. The Fibonacci sequence is *1 1 2 3 5 8 13 21 34 55* and so on."

"So, what do the numbers 3 5 18 and 14 mean?" Declan asked puzzled. "Do you think this pattern represents a linguistic code of some kind?"

"It is possible. What if the numbers represent where the letters are positioned in the alphabet starting with the letter *a* being number 1?"

Declan scribbled down the alphabet. "Let's see, 3 5 18 14 would spell out *C-E-R-N*."

"That's no English word. Could it be Latin or Italian?"

"I bet Mom could help, Dalya. She's the expert linguist who understands Latin and other ancient languages. You know, I've been thinking about what you said back at the maze. Maybe we should explain the truth to Mom and Dad. They deserve to know about our powers. I think that once they know our story, they could really help us. Together, we could be a good team."

"Yes, Declan, but you've made a good point regarding Mom and Dad's safety. I mean, once we tell them, there is no going back to the way their lives have been before."

"That's right. I still feel that way, but in the end we are a family, which means they are already involved and in danger just by being connected to us. It's fair to tell them as soon as possible."

"Let's go and tell them right now," Dalya said, relieved.

From under their parents' door, a weak light escaped into the hallway. Declan knocked on the door with his sister at his side. Mom opened the door, looking tired. Both Mr. and Mrs. Salk had papers strewn all over the two small wooden tables in the room. Mr. Salk was working on architectural drawings for his current construction project. Mrs. Salk was studying music notes for an upcoming choir concert.

"Hi darlings, it's 10:30 now. What are you doing at this hour? We thought you had already gone to bed." She invited them in and closed the door.

Dad wearily looked up from his work and murmured, "Hello Dalya, hello Declan. Are you guys all right?"

The twins answered in perfect synchronization, "Yes,

Dad. We're fine."

They gave each other a surprised look. Even they were shocked at how freakishly similar they could be sometimes.

"Can we do anything for you, honey?" Mom asked, directing her question at Declan.

"Uh, yes Mom. Could you please translate something for us? These words here." He handed her a slip of paper with the letters *C-E-R-N* and the words *NIHIL RESPONSUM*.

Mrs. Salk looked at the message and within a second she told them, "Oh yes. It's Latin. *NIHIL* means *nothing*. *RESPONSUM* means *answer*. The whole message means *nothing is the answer*."

"Thanks, Mom, how about these four letters?"

"*C-E-R-N?*" She paused. "It isn't Latin." She sat down at her small wooden table, picked up a pencil, and began scribbling notes on a blank edge of an Italian newspaper. "I believe this is an acronym."

"What do you mean, Mom?" inquired Declan.

Dad raised his head while he cleared his throat. "There is a European organization called CERN."

Mom added, "Right! It stands for *Conseil Européen pour la Recherche Nucléaire*. It is French for the *European Council on Nuclear Research*."

"What exactly is this organization about?" Dalya asked.

Both twins' curiosity was peaked again.

"Yes, now we are getting into my interests," Dad piped up. "Well, CERN is a group of scientists from around the world who conduct physics experiments at a special underground science laboratory and facility shared by Switzerland and France. CERN was established in 1952 by twelve European countries. Switzerland and eleven other countries formed a committee which decided to plan and build the world's most complex physics laboratory ever. They created a powerful machine that could make subatomic particles travel near the speed of light. It's called the Large Hadron Collider, and it's the largest machine of its kind, a circular twenty-seven kilometer long tunnel built a hundred meters underground. Now, when particles or matter collide into each other, new matter called *tachyons* or *neutrinos* would be formed. This matter could create black holes, time travel, worm holes, and even invisibility."

Dad stopped to let the twins absorb these words before he continued. Declan and Dalya felt astonished about the reference to invisibility.

"In 2008, scientists announced to the world they were able to produce tachyons for the first time."

Declan anxiously asked, "Dad, have they truly discovered any of these things? What about invisibility?"

"Well, to this day, they cannot be sure if what they found was accurate. Scientists are trying to repeat the experiment, but it hasn't worked as of yet. But who knows?"

"Incredible!" interrupted Dalya.

"Do you mean they don't know for sure if the tachyons really exist?"

"That's correct, Declan. In fact, some believe that

the machine will never produce these subatomic particles again."

"What's your opinion, Dad?" Dalya asked.

Mr. Salk thought hard for a minute. With his left hand, Dad rubbed his chin as he sat on his chair, his eyes focusing intensely on something across the room. He turned and smiled at the twins. "I think anything is possible. People have invented some amazing technologies, which have allowed us to achieve incredible feats. We have built spaceships, traveled to the moon, built high structures, invented robots, and constructed tools to do just about any kind of work we can imagine. Now we have the technological capacity to build machines smaller than a human cell. If we can do these things now, then it's possible that we can find ways to travel through time and to make objects and people invisible."

The twins slowly turned to each other, nodded their heads, and gave each other reassuring smiles.

Declan began, "Dad, Mom, we have something very important to tell you."

Dalya inhaled slowly and held her breath. "We have the power to become invisible."

Mr. and Mrs. Salk withheld an impulse to overreact. The couple's eyes met, maintaining each other's gaze. Everyone was silent and still. The twins couldn't bear the silence as Mom and Dad each internally figured out what to say next.

Dad responded first, "What an incredible thing. How do you know for sure?"

"Shall we demonstrate?" Dalya suggested.

"Sure, honey. Go ahead," Mom responded.

Both twins commanded softly, "Invisible." They dematerialized.

"Well, what do you think?" Dalya asked.

Mrs. Salk gasped. She did not know in which direction she should speak. "We think this is fantastic."

"Spectacular! How did you come upon this power?" asked Dad.

Mr. and Mrs. Salk were eager to learn about the new phenomenon their children presented to them.

"How we discovered our powers is a long story. Please sit down, and we'll tell you everything," directed Declan.

"How about I make us some tea?" Mom offered. In the kitchenette, she prepared the tea bags and a pot of water. The twins rematerialized and told their story with dramatic liveliness, beginning with the sinkhole discovery, the chase in Paris, the turf maze encounter, and all the rest. For an hour, the parents sat patiently listening and watching the twins explain their recent experiences until the animated siblings eventually finished the narrative.

Mr. and Mrs. Salk asked a myriad of questions about their ordeal. The storytellers answered them as best as they could. "We know very little about how our invisibility works and why exactly this SOUP group wants us," summarized Declan.

"We still don't really know how our gizmos work. After a lot of trial and error, we got them to work by accident."

"Well, my darlings, let's figure out what will happen next with CERN, shall we?"

"Yes Mom. I believe that our invisibility and the CERN physics center are connected in some way," answered Declan.

"Tomorrow, we will make some calls to organize a visit."

"Thanks Dad. Maybe they could help us learn more about our powers," Dalya said.

"I would like to know how long these powers will stay with us," Declan commented.

Dad, feeling tired as the midnight hour approached, muttered, "Yes, these are all good inquiries that must have answers. Let's all go to bed and get some sleep. We'll get up early tomorrow, eat a hearty breakfast, and enjoy the sights here. The day after, we'll take a plane to Switzerland."

✦

The next morning, Mr. Salk had called the facility and arranged all the flights and the car rental. The following day, they flew out of Venice in the early afternoon. Four hours later, they arrived in Geneva. The family anticipated an enlightening visit and hoped to learn more about their predicament. They were not aware of the two fake taxi cabs following them as they left the Geneva Cointrin airport to make the short drive to Meyrin. The SOUP agents stayed back and decided not to apprehend the unaware travelers until later.

In Paris, they were ready to catch the twins and bring them to their hidden science labs. Why did they wait now? What change of plan did SOUP hatch?

8 Tachyons ✦

"Haaa, haaa…" Dalya softly exhaled several breaths onto the rental jeep's window while her dad steered the vehicle to the CERN complex. She observed her circular breath prints that condensed and evaporated from their glass medium. They drove up to one of the three ground-level entrances that led to the complex. A slim middle-aged man immediately approached the family as they were exiting from the car.

"Are you the Salk family?" he asked impatiently with a French accent.

"Why, yes we are. May I ask who you are, please?" Mr. Salk questioned suspiciously.

Patiently, the twins just observed, turning their heads to look around for any intruders. The vulnerable siblings suspected SOUP agents to pop out of their loud helicopters at anytime. They imagined men in black attire repelling swiftly onto the ground to ensnare them into a trap. Rapidly, the captives would be taken away to some unknown location to be questioned for their valuable secrets. Fortunately, this dangerous scenario didn't play out.

"My name is Michel Pascal. For some time, I have

acted as one of the leading project managers here, focusing on the Hadron Collider activities. Before we go any further, I need to know that you are who you say you are. Do you have picture identification?" Mr. Pascal asked.

The four visitors handed their passports to him. The Frenchman checked them carefully and quickly handed the booklets back to the owners. He worked efficiently and minimized any unnecessary waste of his time.

"I still need to ask you some questions before you enter the complex. You do want to enter, don't you?" he asked, seeming to enjoy taunting the family.

"Yes, we would very much like to learn about this place," Declan insisted politely, hoping to remain on the man's good side.

"First question," the efficient man began, "*Liber*...?" He trailed off.

"*Abaci*," Dalya chimed in.

Mr. Pascal smiled and replied, "Good, next question: *Nihil*...?"

"*Responsum*," Declan bleated out.

"Excellent," the man responded. "Now, one more test before I allow you to step inside and continue your odyssey. What is the name given to a collection of special sticks used as a calculation device for over three hundred years, before the electronic calculator was invented? A hint, if you will: your body's frame is a clue."

The family remained silent while thinking about Mr. Pascal's question.

Dalya then said, "Bones. Our body's frame is the

skeleton, which is made out of our bones." She smirked at the man and confidently replied, "Napier's Bones. John Napier of sixteenth century Scotland invented *Napier's bones*, a system to calculate complex arithmetic operations. He also popularized the use of the decimal point in Europe, among other things." Dalya beamed with pride.

"Fantastic, young lady. You have certainly earned your entrance into our wondrous tunnels. Very impressive indeed," he said with elation, chuckling away as he guided the family toward the entrance.

The twins and their parents were relieved, displaying nervous smiles of agreement toward a satisfied Mr. Pascal. They went quickly inside the building.

"We'll take the lift downward," the host politely instructed.

Black lighting illuminated the darkened elevator as they speedily descended further and further down into the earth's interior. After an abrupt stop, the Mr. Pascal cordially escorted the visitors out, leading them into a facility that housed the most spectacular collection of advanced machines ever built by human hands.

The facility's appearance took on the effect of the most elaborate science fiction movie one could ever imagine. Machines of all sizes and shapes were busy at work, humming and beeping all around the visitors and their host. The twins stretched their necks like two perched owls scanning for their nocturnal food. Their surroundings amazed them.

Mr. Pascal spoke pleasantly. "Do you know why you are here?"

"No, not really. But we would like to learn more about your invisibility experiments," answered Declan.

"And why are you so interested?" Mr. Pascal inquired.

"Well. You know who we are, don't you? I mean, you know what we are about and the special things we can do, right?" questioned Dalya.

Mr. Pascal smiled and nodded his head.

Dalya then added seriously, "We want answers."

"Well, maybe you'll get your answers."

"We hope so, Mr. Pascal," Mom interjected.

He then lectured, "At this underground level, we have accelerator machines performing various experiments. We want to know how the universe began. Down here we try to recreate the big bang on a small scale, the explosion that took place 13.8 billion years ago which created our universe."

Declan inquired, "You mean these machines are supposed to create a new universe?"

"Something of that nature. You see, if we could replicate the big bang, we will have a better idea of the hidden material our universe is made of. Therefore, we would be able to travel through time, create black holes, and—"

"Make objects invisible," Dalya eagerly interrupted.

"Yes, that is correct. We know that if we can make atomic particles crash into each other, moving near or at the speed of light, we'll see stuff we've never seen before. It is like crashing rocks together. The rocks break apart and little pieces fly everywhere. However, with atoms something else happens. New material or matter is revealed. These new materials are called *neutrinos* or *tachyons*. Tachyons hold the key to understanding everything about us, the universe's beginnings."

Dalya asked, "Are you close to solving this puzzle, Mr. Pascal?"

"We are very close indeed. Some of my top scientists say we are just hours away. You have arrived at the right moment to possibly witness this most important and extraordinary discovery. Please, right this way."

He led them to a golf cart which took them through a long brightly lit tunnel. Machines were everywhere with scientists attending to them. A maze of tunnels stretched like long tentacles in different directions. Some machines were six stories high and a football field long with rays shooting through their transparent tubes.

For several minutes, they drove through the amazing complex and eventually came to a halt. In front of them was a blue tube about five meters in circumference.

Mr. Pascal formally announced, "May I present to you the Large Hadron Collider." The blue tube hummed and made swishing sounds as if a locomotive train was jetting through the tube at constant, repetitive intervals.

"Here is where we make atomic particles collide. My dear friends, tomorrow we expect an important discovery. Your questions about your invisible powers may be answered. We invite you to spend the night with us in one of our visitor's residences. Would this be possible, Mr. and Mrs. Salk?"

The parents looked at the twins. Dad asked with a

smile, "What do you think?"

"Definitely!" the twins responded harmoniously.

"Very well, my assistant will guide you to your room and be of service to you. A vehicle will come to retrieve you in the morning and bring you to our facility's central control room. I will see you tomorrow."

After finishing his instructions, Mr. Pascal sped away in the golf cart. Another cart came to pick up the family. An assistant drove them for several minutes through more tunnels. Elaborate matrices of platforms and connecting staircases crisscrossed all around the visitors.

At last, the guests arrived at their spacious high tech apartment. It was designed to keep out any sounds. The dwelling had a bathroom, kitchen, living room, dining room, a den, and three other rooms that could be used for bedrooms, offices, or for other purposes. It was obvious to the visitors that this apartment was designed for long-term stays. Residents were protected from any type of fallout due to slow radioactive leaks or explosions.

That night, the family slept soundly, oblivious to all of the activity surrounding them from the floors above and below them. They woke up at around seven o'clock the next morning, took turns showering, and dressed while working the cobwebs out of their heads.

Soon thereafter, the doorbell rang. Mr. Salk opened the door. A worker silently entered the room with a wheeled, multilevel shelf that was filled with food and drinks. Breakfast was served. From the living room wall, the phone rang. Mr. Pascal explained to Mr. Salk there would be a vehicle arriving within thirty minutes which will take them to the Large Hadron Collider. Mr. Salk hung up the phone and advised the family to be ready promptly.

The visitors felt excited. Declan and Dalya were especially anxious to finally learn about the source of their powers. Never would they have imagined there was a connection between the secrets of the universe and this incredible place. The family waited outside their quarters. From a long corridor, a driver with her golf cart arrived and carried them away through an illuminated tunnel.

The tunnel became gradually darker and quieter as they drove deeper into it. They traveled to a more remote area of the compound. Tubes and pipes overlaying the tunnel's interior became apparent. They had arrived at the Large Hadron Collider's command center. From this point, atomic particles would be sent through the twenty-seven kilometer long tunnel. The atoms being projected would collide with other atoms and form the explosions that would reveal new matter—matter that holds the various structures of atoms together, the matter that would reveal the secrets of how the universe began within the first second after the big bang explosion.

Mr. Pascal greeted the family with a warm smile as they got out of the cart. "Good morning. I do hope you were treated well."

"Oh yes, we were. Thank you, Mr. Pascal, for your hospitality," Mrs. Salk replied.

"Well, let's get to our purpose, shall we? My scientists have informed me that as of early this morning, they harnessed the elusive tachyon matter." Mr. Pascal invited the family inside the command center. "Look at this monitor. During the experiment, our cameras took thousands of still pictures per second inside of the Large Hadron Collider. The pictures came from different sections and give the observer an image of what has transpired."

"I see greenish-blue worm-shaped objects. What are those things?" Declan excitedly asked.

"Those are the tachyons we have been searching for. Some people refer to them as *Dark Matter*. After forty years of experimenting, we have finally found one of the biggest secrets of how our universe began," Mr. Pascal said with satisfaction and excitement. "You see, we believe the universe started from nothing, meaning hidden matter, and then exploded. We call this explosion the big bang. Everything we see today—stars, planets, galaxies—everything comes from this big bang. The sand and soil on our planet comes from this enormous explosion. We, our bodies, come from the dust of the earth created during the birth of our universe. Now we are seeing the tachyons, the first material, the hidden building blocks that constitute the universe and all the objects in it."

The dramatic host allowed his audience to digest this information.

A moment later, Dalya asked, "You mean these worm-shaped tachyons are the beginnings of all life?"

"Yes, that is correct, young lady," the man confirmed with a smile. "The tachyons may also be the source of invisibility."

"Does your experiment have any link with the Project Rainbow that went on many years ago?" inquired Declan.

The host felt surprised. "No, not directly. How do you know about Project Rainbow?"

"Someone told us about it while we traveled through Italy," stated Dalya.

Suddenly a muffled *crash* sounded a short distance away. Emergency sirens began to wail frantically, signaling intruders had entered the compound. Flashing red lights accompanied the deafening sirens.

Wasting no time, Mr. Pascal ordered, "Quick, get into the golf cart, and I will personally drive you to a safe exit area. You must not be captured."

"Yes, we know. A woman named Kate met us in Paris and told us all about the SOUP group's plan to detain us!" explained Dalya.

"Kate, you have seen *Kate*?"

"Why, yes. We barely escaped from SOUP," explained Declan.

In astonishment, Mr. Pascal whispered to himself, "Kate, oh…Kate."

He stared in front of himself for a few seconds until Dalya brazenly interrupted his thoughts.

"Hey, let's get out of here, Mr. Pascal. Pay attention."

Snapping out of his trance, the Frenchman regained his composure and replied, "Yes, of course." He pressed the foot pedal and off they went, back in the direction they had come. Explosions rocked the compound, violently disrupting operations throughout the entire complex. Smoke began to fill the corridor as they approached the main square of the compound, not far from where the family had slept. The golf cart weaved around panicked people, who were running here and there. SOUP must have entered the compound and sabotaged the place. They had covertly planted bombs all around and set them on intermittent timed detonations.

Perspiring while breathing excitedly, Mr. Pascal instructed, "Now, listen to me very carefully, everyone. You must go back to your residence. There, you will find a secret vaulted door on the living room floor. Open it and follow the tunnel out of here. It will lead you to a safe destination. And don't worry yourselves because someone will rendezvous with you when you reach the location."

"What will happen to you?" asked Dalya.

"I must stay here to secure and seal off the Large Hadron Collider from the intruders. I have my own escape passage to exit through. I have something for you, Dalya." With trembling hands, Mr. Pascal retrieved a metal tubular container. He slipped it into Dalya's hands.

"Here is a message with a map. I was going to give it to you later. Please take it. The map will lead you to a location that will reveal more information about your and Declan's powers. Now go, children. Hurry!" he commanded.

Without hesitation, the family followed instructions and departed speedily. Declan and Dalya ducked into their apartment first, not wanting to be captured by the ominous group. Before the parents entered the residence, they took one last look around. People were running in all directions. Machines and equipment exploded everywhere. Automatic ceiling sprinklers sprayed their specialized chemicals to douse the fires. Equipment was falling from the upper levels while some machines randomly spit out electric sparks and cackled. The tunnel lights flickered and many burned out, leaving various areas of the compound in complete darkness.

"C'mon! Let's go!" Mr. Salk barked to his overwhelmed wife. They swallowed hard, ran into the apartment, and closed the door. The family was safely tucked inside from all the chaos. The pandemonium outside their door was met with silence from inside their room. Dad opened the living room's cellar door. Dim red lights revealed a built-in ladder about five meters deep, which led to an underground path. They climbed down, anxious to leave behind the destruction and turmoil above them.

"Is this all happening because of us?" Dalya asked as her voice shook from her running through the tunnel.

"I'm afraid so Dalya," Declan responded. The twins took off running ahead of their parents through the tunnel.

Mr. and Mrs. Salk were ready to run off when suddenly they heard a voice above in the room.

"Wait, you must wait," someone yelled from above.

"Mr. Pascal? It is you. Are you okay?" asked Mrs. Salk, completely taken aback.

"What are you doing here?" Mr. Salk abruptly

questioned, feeling shocked.

"I must insist that you do something for me. Please take this special case," Mr. Pascal urgently requested. "I'm sorry. There's no time to explain everything in detail. Follow the written directions inside the case. Don't let anyone take it from you. When the time is right, you will know who to give it to. Thank you and goodbye."

After depositing the case into Mr. Salk's hands, Mr. Pascal rushed away. The bewildered parents gave each other a quick worried look and ran into the tunnel to catch up to the twins.

The family ran endlessly through the dark, echoing passage. What will they find at the tunnel's end?

9 Qarahunge ✦

Stomp, stomp! With every running step the family members put distance between themselves and the complex. The damp tunnel stretched its limb onward for two kilometers until it revealed its outlet. After fifteen minutes, they could finally see the sun's radiance at the end of the tunnel. A silhouetted figure stood still just outside the exit.

Dad yelled, "Wait! Who is standing there?"

The escapees suddenly stopped.

"Is it someone who can help us? Or could it be a SOUP agent?" Mom asked breathing heavily.

The twins fell silent while they observed the figure. Just then, the figure hollered, "Dalya, Declan, is that you in there?"

"Are you Kate?" responded Dalya.

"Yes, it's me. I'm here to guide you to your next destination. Come quickly. We don't have much time because SOUP will soon find this tunnel and follow us."

Kate's voice echoed through the tunnel. The twins rushed toward her, followed by Mr. and Mrs. Salk. Dalya arrived first and ran into Kate's arms.

"It's so good to see you, Kate. I thought SOUP

might have discovered your identity." Dalya's eyes gleamed with joyous relief.

"I'm so happy you've stayed clear of danger. Listen to me carefully. There's a vehicle over there in this forest"—she pointed with her index finger— "It will take us to the Lausanne Airport La Blécherette."

"Where are we flying to?"

"There's no time for questions now, Dalya. Let's get to the airplane. On our flight, I will answer your queries the best I can. Come on everyone, let's depart from this place."

The parents nodded and ran behind Kate and the children to a large four-wheel-drive jeep. They piled in, and the vehicle roared away, leaving the sabotaged facility permanently behind.

Its passengers observed the snowcapped Alps to the south of Lake Geneva as they drove the seventy kilometer stretch through snowy vineyards. While they traveled, a strange feeling stirred inside Dalya. Her heart began to beat faster as her breathing rhythm became shallow and quicker. Beads of sweat formed at her hairline, and she felt a hot sensation that welled up inside her body. Images began flashing in her mind, accompanied by many different colors that swirled around with spiraled shapes. She closed her eyes and concentrated on the pictures being projected. Constellations appeared, various circular stone structures, the sun, the moon, spiral galaxies, numbers, a crater, stone temples, a circular calendar, and other mysterious objects danced around, floating toward and away from her mind's eye like dancing puppets dangling to and fro from their strings. The number zero glowed repeatedly between the other images. Her eyes slowly reopened but with an empty, glazed expression in them.

Dalya's trance-like facial expression alarmed her brother.

He nudged her with his elbow and said, "Sis? Are you all right? Wake up, Dalya, come out of it."

With Declan's concerned prodding, she blinked her eyes rapidly and shook her head to release herself from the hypnotic trance, feeling as though she was emerging from a deep sleep. After several seconds, she was behaving normally again.

"I've never seen you like that before, Dalya. What happened to you?"

"I'm not sure. Since we've had our invisible powers, there have been other times I've felt the same as I do now, but the sensations were never this strong before. For the fourth time now, I have dreamed of different images. There must be some meaning or purpose behind these visions, a message of some kind."

"A message? What kind of message?"

"I don't know. Maybe Kate will have some answers."

"Let me ask her something first."

"Kate?" Declan interrupted, "How did you know where to find us again?"

She smiled. "We at SOUP have certain devices that help us track anyone we want to find. No one can ever hide from us for long." She finished with a devilish grin to dramatize her point and to fool with Declan and his sister. The twins began to feel deeply concerned.

Kate then comforted them, "I'm just trying to be humorous, even though what I've said about SOUP is true. However, the reason why I'm here is that I've been sent by the other group."

"Does that mean SOUP will eventually catch us?" asked Declan.

Silence filled the jeep as everyone pondered the unthinkable.

Dalya broke the silence. "I have some questions I would like to ask you about our next—"

"Again, let's discuss your questions while we are aboard the plane. We'll have more time and will be less distracted in the air. Plus, we could encounter SOUP while we are still on the ground. During the flight, we'll be a lot safer from them."

Dalya bit her lip, as she was fervent to learn about her images and all of the incredible events that she and her brother had experienced during the past two weeks.

"Well, all right," she responded, feeling disappointed.

Passing the city of Lausanne, they approached the airport. Three SOUP helicopters flew quickly toward them from behind. The same crew from the Paris assault was onboard. Loud motors, twirling blades, and babble from communication radios all operated to achieve their iron-clad purpose—to capture the twins. The crew was preparing their gear. The man with the jingling keys sat up front next to the pilot of the lead helicopter. He was giving directions and barking orders to the other men regarding preparations. Jeep met airplane. The family spilled out of the vehicle. Kate, who quickly led them into a private jet, started its engines.

"You can fly this plane?" Mr. Salk asked, surprised.

"Besides being a scientist, I'm a trained military pilot, Mr. Salk. Don't worry. I'll be the co-pilot today. You are safe in the air with me," Kate responded with a confident tone backed by a quick smile. The passengers felt reassured with this answer and hurriedly buckled themselves into the cushioned chairs. Afterward, the driver, who was now the main pilot, and Kate strapped themselves in. They flicked switches and pushed buttons to prepare the plane for its departure. The airplane's engines were specially designed for quick departure thrusts, allowing for the jet's sleek body to conduct quick turns and twists. It was the perfect getaway plane.

The malignant sounds of rotary blades slicing the air became louder with every passing second.

Kate ordered, "Take off, Mr. Pasteur!"

He then placed his hand on the accelerator lever and pushed it forward. Hissing sounds of the jet's idling engines suddenly roared to life. The plane jerked forward and sped down the runway while the twins looked out of the thick windows next to them. The helicopters were flying right at them. One hunter flew behind the plane, and the other two machines speedily swooped down toward each side of the escaping aircraft. The jet and its tense passengers were surrounded.

As Declan peered out of the window, one helicopter's door slid open. Two men sat on the open door ledge. One agent swung his body around toward the jet, holding a small, shoulder-mounted cannon device.

Declan suddenly yelled, "There's a cannon pointed right at us, he's going to—" He couldn't finish his sentence. The plane rocked as a force of air engulfed it.

"Thumper guns!" Kate shrieked.

"More like a thumper cannon!" Declan corrected loudly. The sturdy jet was not hampered by the first air blast. *Bam!* A second air wave rocked the plane, causing the right landing gear to rise off the ground, tilting the plane. Dalya and Mrs. Salk yelped in surprise. Mr. Salk gave off a small holler of shock. Mr. Pasteur kept the forward thrust lever at full speed. The engines defiantly roared against a third blast that shook the plane.

"Hmm," the boss grunted from his seat. "The first blast should have slowed them down. They must have a specially designed airplane." Pondering the situation for a brief moment, he then abruptly ordered all three teams, "Our thumper cannons were ineffective. Switch to grappling hooks. I repeat, switch to grappling hooks, now!"

The three helicopters shifted their positions and aimed their small grappling guns at the jet from three different angles.

"Fire!" The titanium steel claws with their attached cables hurled themselves through the air. The claws, hungry to latch their jaws onto something, immediately found the landing gear, slowing down the jet plane. The boss was pleased. "Remember to be careful, everyone. The children should not be harmed. We need our precious cargo alive. Just stop the plane, understood?" He loudly barked into his radio microphone to overpower the helicopter's deafening engines.

"We're slowing down! Do something, Kate. Get us out of here, quick!" beseeched Dalya.

"Just let me concentrate!"

The helicopter pilots slowed their engines to pull on the cables to stop the plane. Before the third helicopter pulled back, Dalya could see the front passenger. He wore navigator sunglasses. His lips were moving as he held the radio microphone close to his mouth.

"He must be the boss, the one who is after us," she mumbled. Mrs. Salk shrieked, "That's the guy from the gas company who was asking questions about you guys. To think, I even allowed him to inspect our backyard!"

A second before the three helicopters could tighten their cables, Kate flicked open a plastic cover with her right-hand thumb.

"Brace yourselves everyone. Here we go!" she warned loudly. Inhaling deeply, she pressed a red button between the two pilot seats. *Swooooosh*! The jet lurched forward with breakneck accelerating thrust. Both pilots and passengers were pressed hard against their seats. Mr. Pasteur struggled to keep his sweaty hands on the vibrating steering mechanism. Two of the helicopters' cables snapped instantly, sending the machines spinning like tops over the airstrip. One helicopter crashed to the ground. The second one spun around as it rose into the sky and disappeared out of sight. Shortly thereafter, the twirling black body finally steadied itself and landed on a field further away. Its passengers poured out of the aircraft, feeling dizzy and disoriented.

The man with the keys was the first to recover. As soon as his wits were intact, he immediately grabbed the helicopter's radio and barked orders to another SOUP team for assistance.

Meanwhile, the jet roared down the airstrip, picking up speed. The third helicopter relentlessly clung on to the plane with its grappling hook.

"Will the helicopter prevent us from clearing those mountains ahead?" Mom asked in a tremulous, concerned tone.

Kate shouted, "At our current speed, we could get over them. However, with the extra dragging weight of that helicopter we may not have enough thrust."

"We will, Kate. You can do it," Declan responded.

The mountains ahead were twelve thousand meters away. Crucially needed distance was also cut short by a large forest, which stood between the plane and the Alps. Two more minutes, and they would crash into the forest at their current speed. Or they could stop the plane while taking the awfully big risk of escaping on foot.

"We need to unhook that helicopter somehow," Declan shrieked.

"Close the left rear landing gear, Mr. Pasteur!" Kate ordered.

"We need the wheels for support. If I close them, we'll crash."

"No! We are still moving fast enough at take-off speed. Since we have enough lift, the other wheels can support us. Now do it!"

The pilot flicked a switch on his window side. Wheels entered first, and then the door attempted to close. The cable blocked the door.

"Try it again!" Kate barked.

Mr. Pasteur tried several more times. The door repeatedly bit down on the cable as it attempted to shut, fraying the cable until it was finally cut. Giving up its locking hold on the landing gear, the cable retreated into the air. The helicopter whirled around and then skidded along some grass. It bounced up and down a few times; its long rotary blades struck the runway and broke apart, sending their flailing blade bits all over. One blade hit the plane's underbelly but no damage was done. Cheers filled the jet's cabin. The pilot steered the plane upward. The mountains stretched their rocky, solid paws into the sky to grasp the plane, but to no avail. The plane cleared the peaks by just a few meters and roared into the morning sky toward its furtive destiny.

✦

"Where are you taking us?" asked Mrs. Salk.

"I was instructed to fly you to the capital city Yerevan in Armenia. That's all I know. The twins have further information."

Puzzled, the twins eyed each other. Dalya remembered. From her jeans pocket, she grabbed a tube.

"Mr. Pascal gave it to me before we parted ways. He mentioned there was a message inside." With quiet anticipation, Dalya opened the container and untied the cloth string which bounded a scroll. She patiently spread the paper out to its full length. The twins slowly read and studied the information on the paper which displayed a hand-drawn map. There were unfamiliar symbols and writings on the map and along the scroll's edges. The number zero was inscribed, accompanied by the words *NIHIL RESPONSUM*.

Declan said, "*NIHIL RESPONSUM*. The same phrase we've seen before."

"Nothing is the— oh gosh! Instead of *nothing is the answer* this message probably means *zero is the answer*. Zero keeps appearing whenever those images swarm into my mind, just like before. I believe that the message refers to zero. Also, think about Fibonacci and his work regarding the number zero."

"Are you sure, Dalya?"

"I'm quite certain." She studied the rest of the message. "Look at this. Besides our Latin phrase the word *Qarahunge* keeps showing up in these writings. Do you know what that means, Declan?"

"Qarahunge is in Armenia. I read a book on ancient mysteries that cited Qarahunge as a prehistoric stone structure of some kind, which might have acted as a star map that somehow tracked the constellations. The stars' movements could show how long it takes the Earth to revolve around the sun. According to the book, some people say it was also a way for Qarahunge's builders to track the sun and moon's movements in order to tell time within a day. Years, months, and weeks could be calculated to keep track of time over hundreds or even thousands of years. Even hours, minutes, and seconds could be figured out. Humanity's first calendar could have come from various ancient cultures which inhabited Qarahunge or other, similar sites located all over the world."

"You mean different people from all over the planet had similar stone structures like this one?" asked Dalya.

"Yes. Interesting isn't it?" Declan grinned. "How could different people from all over the planet have the same knowledge thousands of years ago? Separated by oceans and vast distances, ancient peoples had no airplanes, cars, or trains to visit each other. Proper boats for world voyages didn't exist yet. How is it that people who have never met each other were able to build stone structures that shared common features?"

Dalya dove into silent contemplation.

Declan added, "To this day, no one can answer this question. And no one even knows who built Qarahunge, or other stone structures, like Stonehenge in England, or the ancient ruins of Cuzco in Peru, South America."

"Let's tell Kate to take us to Qarahunge."

Declan eyed his sister deeply. He then addressed the co-pilot. "Kate, could you take us to Qarahunge? We believe something important is there for us."

Kate turned backwards to face the twins. "Now, I understand. I'm familiar with Qarahunge. It's located one hundred fifty-five miles from Yerevan, just outside the city of Sisian. To reach your destination, we must complete a four day trek through the desert."

"Why don't we just rent a car and drive there from

Yerevan?" Declan asked.

"I recommend we minimize our contact with others. We should not rent vehicles and avoid the city's people to prevent witnesses of knowing our whereabouts. We shouldn't make it easy for SOUP to find us. We must maintain a low profile. We'll have to visit a market and buy a few supplies to set up camp in the desert. This will expose us a bit, but there is no other way to get supplies."

"They would even follow us to distant Asia?"

"Yes, Dalya. SOUP is a tenacious, sinister group."

✦

The pilot radioed the city's airport control tower for permission to land the plane on a private landing strip.

"Do you know anything special about Qarahunge, Kate?" Dalya and Declan inquired.

"Well, there are over two-hundred erect stone structures which are quite remarkable to look at. During my investigations on previous projects, I have repeatedly seen photos showing sections of this site. No one is exactly sure who built the odd standing sentries."

"Declan, I believe the images I experienced since we discovered the sinkhole come from this site somehow."

"Does the thought make you feel uncomfortable?" asked Declan.

"A little bit. I mean, we don't know what's going to happen to us once we find this Qarahunge place."

"Well, since the sinkhole, I too have experienced special sensations," Declan whispered intensely. "It's hard to describe, but I think some kind of force is protecting us. Every time SOUP nearly catches us, we somehow manage to escape at the last moment."

"I hadn't thought of that, but you're right. Maybe we're meant to discover something really important about our powers."

"It seems that everything we've experienced since we discovered the sinkhole is for some important reason."

Dalya silently sat, thinking about the profound words her brother had just spoken.

At late afternoon, the plane landed smoothly, leaving a dust trail swept up by the dry wind as the jet slowed to a complete stop. Mr. and Mrs. Salk had already awakened from their slumber a few minutes before landing. It was December 17, four days before the winter solstice in the Earth's Northern Hemisphere. The passengers opened the exit door and slowly stepped onto the short ladder that deposited them onto Armenia's orange-brown soil. Armenia's climate is cold; its desert region is isolated with barren flats stretching in every direction.

The travelers bought some food, water, and camping supplies from a local merchant and set off into the desert. After a few hours of walking, a caravan of horses and people wearing lightly colored robes walked toward them. Mr. Pasteur reacted by calmly greeting them in a local Armenian dialect. He chatted amiably while chuckling and joking with the wanderers. At the end of their conversation, he then gratefully thanked them for their kindness.

Mr. Pasteur then turned to his group and announced,

"These people are Armenian natives who are part of a nomadic tribe and have offered to guide us to Qarahunge. We will eat what is offered, and tomorrow morning they will trek with us to the site."

Kate thanked Mr. Pasteur for his translation and help. The hospitable nomads began to unload their supplies off their horses' backs. The weary men worked at sorting the supplies while the women and children set out blankets on the desert floor to prepare the evening meal. Makeshift cloth tents were pitched, leavened plates set, and drinks were poured. The Salk family and the pilots were cordially invited by the shaman to join him for dinner in his tent. Everyone sat in a large circle, about twenty people in total. The delicious food filled the traveler's bellies.

Mr. Pasteur asked for everyone's attention. "The shaman will now speak to us about the ancient site." The tribal elder spoke as everyone listened closely to Mr. Pasteur's translation. "The shaman says that they believe the site to be holy. It has been a sacred site for many generations over four thousand years. According to their revered legends, mysterious people built the site and then taught their ancestors the purpose of the construction. He says these people are known as *The Mirifici*."

The shaman stopped speaking to gather his thoughts. "He says we should sleep now. Tomorrow morning, we pack everything onto the horses and make our way to the site to be there before the sun sets on the winter solstice. Only then will we understand Qarahunge's sacrosanct mysteries." Everyone rose to their feet.

✦

Early the next morning, Kate approached the family. "SOUP has contacted me to report to their headquarters. I would like to stay, but I must leave you now. If I don't report back, they'll become suspicious, and this whole expedition will be jeopardized."

"But Kate, we need your help. Please stay," Dalya pleaded.

"We cannot go on without you," Declan insisted.

"Yes, you can. If they are hot on your trail, I will try to lead them astray. Please believe me when I say that I'd rather be with you. Don't worry, you'll be fine. Mr. Pasteur will assist you. You can trust him. Goodbye for now. We'll be in touch."

Kate grabbed some supplies and trekked off into the desert.

The group prepared for its expedition. Horses grunted as their material loads pressed down on their backs while people mounted the animals. The shaman had picked eleven of his best men to accompany the group to Qarahunge.

Mr. and Mrs. Salk dozed off sometimes while they sat on the slow-moving horses. The twins felt the opposite. Their anticipation, curiosity, and a bit of fear made them wide awake and excited about what would be found at the hallowed ancient site.

The caravan, led by the energetic shaman with his wooden staff, rode patiently through the windy, dusty land to Qarahunge. Throughout the journey, during evening camps, the travelers had eaten delicious food and drank strong raw beverages. The Armenian people loved to sing and dance every night after the evening meals. The Salk family and Mr. Pasteur would join in with delight, which allowed them to bond with their desert guides under the twinkling, star-filled sky dominated by Polaris, the North Star. It was the beacon that had navigated the ancient mariners of the world's seas. During the desert journey, the celestial guide had also safely navigated the group. For thousands of years, Polaris was still a reliable comfort for travelers.

✦

Three and a half days later, the caravan arrived at its destination, Qarahunge. The temperature began to drop slowly, and the desert sky gradually transformed into a blend of pinks, oranges, and yellows surrounded by a blanket of dusky blue.

Structures, approximately three meters tall, appeared over a hump in the landscape's horizon. Long jagged rocks stood erect, pointing their leaf-shaped tops straight up toward the heavens. Nothing else supported each rock but its own shape and weight. It looked as if a giant hand had carefully placed them there with a particular purpose.

"Is that the stone temple or structure, Mr. Shaman?" Dalya asked, excitedly waiting for Mr. Pasteur's translation.

The old shaman spoke with a quiet, respectful tone. Mr. Pasteur translated, "He says these rocks are just the first group of stones that lead to the main holy site. In total, there are two hundred and twenty-two large basalt rocks. Each rock can weigh up to—" Mr. Pasteur turned to the elder in midsentence and asked him a question to double-check his translation. "Yes, each rock can weigh up to fifty tons or one hundred thousand pounds."

Declan sat behind his sister on one of the horses and blurted, "Fifty tons. That's quite amazing."

"Each rock weighs as much as a blue whale," Dalya said, impressed.

"He says the two hundred and twenty-two rocks are spread over a half—no, a third—of an imperial mile over this landscape." Mr. Pasteur finished his translation.

The horses lugged onward. Patiently, the animals weaved their way around the eerie-looking stones that loomed over them. The riders felt in awe among these unique stones. Tall, brown-orange guardians pointed to a mysterious place in the darkening sky. The siblings began to feel an emotional connection to this desolate land.

"Dalya, do you feel like we've been here before?"

"It's strange, but yes. How is it possible?"

"I don't know, it's a peculiar yet comforting feeling."

"Where are these stones from? How were they carved? How did people move these giants thousands of years ago without wheeled machines?" Dalya fired off questions at Mr. Pasteur.

"Whoa, slow down, young lady. Nobody knows for certain the answers to your queries. People have asked these questions for many years. The rocks come from mountains far away from here and must have been lifted and placed on something to be transported to this place. Special tools of some kind carved out the circular holes, each about fifteen centimeters in diameter, at the top center of many rocks located here. What ancient devices were used? Nobody has a valid explanation. With all of our modern scientific and technological knowledge today, we still cannot figure out the answers. We just have theories."

"Weren't the Pyramids in Egypt also made from stone quarries found many kilometers away?" asked Declan.

"That's correct. Each stone was perfectly carved into rectangular blocks to form an airtight pyramid. Each individual stone weighed thousands of pounds, and each was lifted to great heights to make those pyramids at Giza."

"There seems to be a pattern between Egypt and here, Mr. Pasteur," Dalya said.

"Please refer to me as Louis. I now sense you are trustworthy and amiable enough for us to be on more personal terms. You are correct. Actually, all over the world there are many archaic pyramids, temples, and other stone structures somehow built with very heavy rocks that were transported from other distant locations."

Declan's curiosity was awakened. "Why didn't people just build these pyramids and temples next to where the rocks were found?"

Louis smiled pleasingly. "Very good question, young man, but nobody really knows. History has not given us any reliable evidence to answer your question."

The shaman interrupted their discussion. As he pointed his dark wrinkled finger ahead, the soft-voiced man suddenly cried out. Louis translated, "There is the center, the most important and cherished location."

At the center, eighty-five large stones stood and formed a circular shape. Each stone had the same unique circular hole as some of the field stones. Inside this eighty five rock circle, there was a concentric circle of about seven meters in diameter made out of two hundred and thirteen small rocks, connected side by side. The twins couldn't contain their curiosity. "Shaman, why are these holes in the large stones?"

Louis translated as the shaman answered, "Our ancestors carved them. At sunset, the sun's beams will radiate through the large eighty-five rocks' holes. Then remarkably, all of the beams will concentrate into one beam at the center of the smaller circle of stones."

"Why is that so important? What happens next?" inquired Dalya.

"*The Mirifici* will give you a gift; a gift only given to selected people. You are the believers."

"Selected for what purpose? How do you know it is us?" replied Declan.

"You say we are believers. What do we believe? What do you mean?" Dalya asked anxiously.

The questions weren't heard anymore as the shaman and his tribal members placed their hands together. Afterward, he closed his eyes and started to chant steadily and peacefully. Obedient tribal members followed his intonations as they kneeled and prayed. As signaled by the beautiful multicolored sky, the sun began to set. Solar beams pierced through the large stones' holes. The eighty-five beams became brighter with each passing minute of the sunset, forming a green-tinted light on the rocks' oval tops.

While everyone witnessed nature's colorful display, Dalya pondered deeply. She suddenly gasped and smiled to herself. Dalya grabbed her brother's arm tightly.

"*Zero is the answer*. The number zero is a symbol for a circle. The circle is here in this small circular stone perimeter or henge. All along, *zero* has been the symbol for this place!" she said resolutely.

"You're right, sis. *Answer* means something important. *Zero is the answer* means the number zero is the essential idea to focus on and to understand. Zero must be related to us and...well...all of this. We just have to figure out what the relevant connection is."

Just before the sun disappeared completely the eighty-five beams joined together and pinpointed a blinding single beam of light onto the center of the small ground circle. The tribal members gasped in delight and awe. Their prayers and chants intensified as the beam illuminated into a greenish-blue color, the same color as the sinkhole light that had enveloped the twins two months ago, and the same color the tachyons revealed at CERN.

"There must be a connection between zero and this place," Dalya repeated to herself, feeling determined to solve this riddle. Unfamiliar sounds emitted from the earth as the beam burned a hole into the ground. A few minutes had passed and the deafening sound pitches nearly drowned out the clamorous Armenian chants. Leather-like wrinkled hands stretched out in front of the natives as they prayed. The nomads showed no signs of being surprised by this powerful yet marvelous light force piercing the earth. They welcomed the light. Gusts of wind whipped around the onlookers while thick thunderous clouds briskly formed above the site. Then the beam suddenly vanished, leaving behind a charred smoky hole.

Feeling cautious, the twins inched slowly toward the hole, taking short and light steps. They leaned over and peered down inside. What they saw was astonishing. From inside the hole, a greenish-blue pulsating glow lit up the twins' faces. A round, metallic, gold-plated object was turning counter-clockwise while it slowly rose from a depth of about twenty-five meters. An inexplicable force slowly pushed the object upward.

Declan, feeling baffled, murmured, "What's happening here?"

The object hummed as it pushed up through the hole. Uncertain of what would happen next, the twins slowly backed away from the action. Clearing the hole, the object rose a meter above the ground and then stopped, hovering in place.

"Incredible, absolutely incredible," Louis whispered.

The shaman stopped praying and walked over to the twins. "Go, my friends, and take the object. You are the chosen ones, who will keep the sacred object safe for all humankind. My ancestors have foreseen this moment thousands of years ago. You must now fulfill your destiny and take the disc to discover your truth and your purpose here on Earth."

The twins felt puzzled by the shaman's words. He looked at them with a warm fatherly expression. "Go now. Take what is rightfully yours," Louis translated.

Dalya turned slowly and looked deeply into the shaman's dark brown eyes.

"Who are *The Mirifici*?"

"In due time, they will reveal themselves. You will see." With these words, he turned and walked back over to the tribal crowd that continued its chants and prayers.

Some rocks reflected the disc's pulsating glow. Taking deep breaths, the twins warily approached the object, reached out their hands, and slowly clenched their fingers to grasp it.

Declan murmured, "Hey sis, why don't you be the first to touch this thing. You deserve it, Dalya."

She looked at her brother with concern, hesitated, and then reached out, placing her fingers on the disc to pull it towards her. Her fingers curled around the object causing the glow to become brighter. Just then, thunder boomed within the churning clouds above. Dusk had nearly arrived, gradually covering the desert with its darkening blanket. Tribal prayers now stopped. Everyone focused on Dalya as she grasped the gold treasure in front of her with outstretched arms. Silence dominated the site.

Dalya and Declan stared at the mysterious disc which displayed a circle at its center. Near it, one could see an engraved ringed planet and an etching of the North Star. A keen observer could make out some circular drawing next to the North Star.

With her fingers, Dalya slowly traced some notches carved into the artifact's edge. She silently counted the notches two times to be sure. There were thirty-six notches all evenly spaced. Then she handed the disc to her eagerly awaiting brother.

Declan savored his turn to analyze the disc. He felt a rush of blood to his head. "This drawing looks very similar to the Mayan Calendar."

He slowly ran his fingers over the smooth, cool surface, feeling every groove of the engraved pictures. Declan turned the treasure over to carefully examine the back. Mysterious letters were inscribed around the entire edge. At the center, a door of some kind with a small circle inside was engraved. The door was made up of a long horizontal line on top and two shorter vertical lines on its sides. Other zigzagged lines decorated the treasure all over its back side.

With a low humming sound, the hole magically sealed itself. The charred soil reverted back to its original earthy brown and orange colors. No trace of the beams or hole could be found. It was as if the entire event had never occurred. The clouds now dissipated, revealing the full starry sky that unfolded above them. Stars stooped so close one could reach out and almost pluck them from the sky. Dalya and Declan looked up to the abundant inventory of stars.

"There is the North Star," Dalya said. "Why is it on

the gold disc? I have a feeling that we are to use it as a guide to get us to our next destination, wherever that may be."

Just then, a tribal man placed his ear onto the ground. He sensed something. Quickly springing to his feet, the tribal man spoke to the shaman, who then spoke with Louis. Louis and the shaman approached the twins.

"We must go now, children. My people detected horses' hooves running toward our direction, less than three kilometers away. Come," begged Louis, translating the elderly man's words.

Declan placed the gold artifact in a pouch slung around his torso. Led by the shaman, the group members hurriedly gathered their things and sped off to a distant rock cluster where they hid. The fear of capture permeated the group.

Meanwhile, over fifty horses and their determined masters swiftly rode until they reached the ancient shrine's center. The thunderous sounds of clomping and pressing hooves pounded the ground. The men jerked on the reins to subdue their animals to stop. Some of the horses moaned and whinnied loudly in resistance until after several seconds they settled down. Large black and brown stallions trotted back and forth around the site. Headlamps shined their beams all over the desert floor. Some men with their infrared goggles scanned the desert and found nothing.

Keys jingled as one horse and its master stood separate from the others to survey the site. The man barked orders for the group to fan out and search the entire area. Horses strode around, their riders searched for the twins. After a while, SOUP and their hired bandits relinquished their search and then abruptly galloped away.

Some time passed after the menacing entourage of SOUP men had disappeared into the desert night until the group decided to come out of hiding.

Back on their horses, Declan and Dalya were already conversing about what to do next. Mr. and Mrs. Salk approached the twins. "Look, we think the jet has been discovered. How else could they have known where to find us?" Mom informed.

"We think it would be better if we did not return to Yerevan and ask these kind folks if they could guide us to the next town. Sisian, wasn't it? Maybe there, we could get to a phone and find some alternative transport out of the desert," suggested Dad.

"Good plan." Declan answered.

✦

The shaman organized lodging and alternative transportation from Sisian to a safe airport.

Just before the family departed from the shaman and his group, they all sadly said their farewells, vowing to see each other again someday.

Declan and Dalya wondered what adventures lay ahead of them. What truths will they uncover with this enigmatic relic?

10 Cahokia ✦

Boom...boom, boom. A pop rock song pulsed out of Declan's headphones which tickled his ears as he lay in bed, watching the sun's morning rays pierce through the bedroom's dust-filled air. The rays reflected off his northern lights poster, loosely pinned on the wall opposite his window. Declan was thinking about what he had experienced in Europe and Asia.

Nearly three months had passed since they discovered the disc in the Armenian desert. The California soil was beginning to warm itself from a mild winter. Declan kept pondering about the medallion he and Dalya had discovered. He worried about his uncertain future to the point where some of his grades spiraled downward. For the most part he liked school, still excelling in his favorite subjects of languages and history. However, he began to neglect his other school subjects he was forced to sit through each excruciating day. Too much was on his mind. Declan hungered for answers.

On December 21, the Northern Hemisphere's winter solstice, the medallion revealed itself to the twins; they wondered what secrets the medallion would expose on the first official day of spring. Therefore, they decided to keep a low profile until then.

After arriving home, the twins hatched a clever scheme to hide the precious disc. They would each be responsible for hiding the medallion for an entire season and not tell the other of its location. A week before an official calendar change of season, the one who had the disc would retrieve it and give it to the other sibling, who would then hide it at a different location for the next three months. These exchanges would continue on indefinitely. With the spring equinox just a few days away, Declan had already handed over the disc to Dalya.

The twins reasoned that the medallion's whereabouts should only be known by one person at a time. They agreed that if the disc's keeper was ever caught, the other sibling would retrieve a coded message placed inside a container hidden in a secret place revealing the relic's location. If both twins were captured, then they would hope to never reveal its location.

As Declan lay in his bed thinking, he noticed that his right hand and arm were beginning to slightly fade in and out. "Funny, I thought I was stabilized. What's going on?" he whispered to himself. After several seconds, the pulsating stopped and all was normal again. Just then, a light tap on the door interrupted him. "Yes, who is it?"

"It's me," a tired morning voice said as Dalya leisurely opened the door. "Dad's ready to go in about five minutes. C'mon, get dressed."

Declan cautiously whispered. "Do you have it?"

"It's right here," Dalya confirmed by opening her jacket to show Declan the inside zipper pocket where the object lay snug against her warm torso. "I'll meet you in the garage."

Declan thought about tomorrow's baseball tryouts and whether he should begin a fifth year in the local baseball league. He was an excellent first baseman and left-armed pitcher, who had led his team to twenty-two victories and one loss last season, allowing the Red Sox to achieve first place in their division. A competitive spirit thrived in him, but most of all he was fond of playing with his teammates and horsing around with them during baseball practices. Declan just loved the game and was a talented athlete. He had even been scouted by the upper division coaches, who asked him to play in last year's all-star league tournament. He pitched a near-perfect game, striking out thirteen of fourteen batters in one of the three games.

Despite his success, Declan was having doubts of playing another season considering how his life had changed in the last several months. Between school and his quest to find answers, Declan wondered if he could dedicate enough time and energy to the sport. Although, after thinking it over, he believed baseball could also be a productive distraction from thinking about SOUP, the medallion, and his uncertain future. Shrugging off his worries, Declan finished dressing and slipped down the stairs.

Dad and the twins piled into the Volvo and drove off. "Well, as we talked about before, I've arranged a meeting between you and an archaeologist friend of mine, Mr. Thomas Hipparchus. He's a retired mathematician and archaeologist from the University of San Polo. Mr. Hipparchus currently works as a construction engineer. However, he still dabbles in ancient mathematics and relics as his hobby. I think he may be able to tell us about the markings on your disc."

"Thank you, Dad, we appreciate your help."

"No problem, Dalya. Your mom and I are here for you."

They drove down a winding road along the California coast, cruising beside an old growth forest, which led them through some foothills of a coastal mountain range. After about an hour's drive, they parked the Volvo in front of an old, wooden home. It resembled a Swiss chalet but without the grazing cows and their ringing bells. The property had a cozy, romantic ambiance comprising of roaming chickens, mangy dogs, and plump dusty cats. Resting on a serene yet remote plateau in the mountains, thick brush and large oaks mostly sealed off the home and its garden from the rest of the world. Odd-looking machines made of simple and complex levers, pulleys, screws, gears, fulcrums, and other mechanical structures stood firmly on the ground around the home.

As the family sprung out of the car, Dalya felt a headache coming on. Unexpectedly, images began to flash through her mind. A military boat, the number zero, and etchings of circles hovered and then sped away from her mind's eye like a school of fish darting away from a diver's field of vision. Dalya winced in pain for a second.

Declan recognized his sister's cringing facial expression from before. As Dalya flinched, he asked, "Is it happening again?"

"Yes, the same images appear, dart around, and then disappear. But I'm fine now. Don't these machines look fascinating?" Dalya wanted to change the subject.

Mr. Salk didn't notice Dalya's pain and replied, "Yes, they are quite unique. Look over there to the left of the house. That's a replica of the first airplane the Wright brothers ever built." The simple aircraft sat motionless, only stirring with small gusts of wind.

"That contraption there to the right of the house is a copy of the first helicopter originally designed by Leonardo Da Vinci."

"Dad, your friend sure likes to build unique things," Dalya commented.

"Yes, Mr. Hipparchus loves to construct machines from ages past. Most of them actually work."

"Look at this Trebujet. It is one of the oldest catapults ever built. It looks fully operational." Declan gleamed

"You may be right."

The three family members walked up some creaky steps leading to a large wooden porch. Mr. Salk banged the oval metal latch several times. No one came. Declan rang the doorbell, which activated a Mozart tune. After a while, the music subsided and several bolt locks were hastily unlatched. A cautious pair of wary blue eyes stared at the three visitors.

The elderly man croaked, "Well, well, Mr. Salk. Good to see you again. How have you been? Oh, and you've brought your lovely children with you to visit me. How wonderful, so wonderful indeed. Please, do come in. I will have to remain inside as my troublesome allergic reactions have kept me sneezing the entire morning. The pollen count feels very high today. Come in, come in."

"Thank you, Mr. Hipparchus. I'm sorry to bother you on a Saturday. As I mentioned on the phone, we've something important we'd like you to look at. This is my daughter Dalya, and my son, Declan."

"Pleased to meet you," Dalya smiled.

"Good to meet you. We hope you can help us," Declan cordially expressed.

"You have a lovely smile, my dear, and you boy, you are a serious one, aren't you?" Mr. Hipparchus said teasingly.

Dad silently nodded to Dalya. She then unzipped her jacket, and took the disc out from her inside pocket. The disheveled gray-haired man looked at the object with utter astonishment.

"Oh my, young lady, what treasure have you got there?" Mr. Hipparchus stared at the golden object, mesmerized at what stood before his tall, thin body.

"Well, Mr. Hipparchus…"

The elderly man piped in, "No, no, my dear. Please call me Thomas. Here, let me have a look at that."

"Well, Thomas, we came upon this artifact, and we would like it analyzed please. Dad said it was possible you could help us determine what this relic is."

"Can you help us, Mr. Hipparchus?" Declan asked urgently.

"Please, everyone, all of you can call me Thomas. It would make things friendlier with our situation here. Young man, would you be kind enough to fetch a pitcher of water from the kitchen and bring some water glasses while I gently prepare this medallion for observation?"

"Uh, sure. No problem." Declan shot a suspicious glance toward Dad.

"Go ahead. It's alright." Dad smiled as the glaring boy went to the kitchen to retrieve the water.

When he returned, Dalya, Dad, and Thomas were already sitting around a worktable that contained mirrors, magnifying glasses, dissecting tools, tweezers, a buffer machine, a metal cutting machine, and a myriad of unfamiliar tools. Thomas' dining room surrounded the worktable. His eating room was actually a converted repair and diagnostic shop. In fact, nearly every part of the house, except for the smelly, cluttered kitchen, was converted into some scientific lab or work center.

Over some years, Thomas became reclusive. Among the surrounding residents, he had the reputation for being eccentric and antisocial. The hermit was a grumpy soul who mainly wanted to be left alone. However, since Thomas didn't hassle anyone and donated generously to the local charities, the residents left him alone. Over sixty years ago, Thomas, who was of Greek descent, had come with his parents to America as a child. Since then, he has lived in this mountain home.

"Now, this looks like a very fascinating artifact, my

dear," he remarked to Dalya. "The designs and markings are quite impressive. The planet Saturn is here. Well, it may be Saturn. Ah, the North Star—Polaris—is indicated here as well."

Thomas then turned the artifact over. He squinted hard at the meticulously constructed etchings. "Well, we have a complex pattern here. It looks like some pre-Columbian calendar or an astronomical marker of some kind."

"I knew it! I thought it might be the Mayan calendar," Declan interjected excitedly.

"Yes, it does look like the Mayan calendar. However, there are some different markings here in the center. In a Mayan calendar, there is a carved face surrounded by four square etchings of animals and other objects enclosed within the squares. Instead of the face at the center, this one has a circle. I have never seen this version of a calendar before, anywhere. Hmm…fascinating. Around the edge are engravings of an ancient language. I believe…wait…could it be? Oh heavens!" Thomas let out a breath and then suddenly got up from his chair.

"What is it?" Declan inquired.

"It cannot possibly be," Thomas uttered as he rushed urgently into the next room, the library.

Silence now dominated the house. The guests waited at the table for the host's return, but he didn't come back for over ten minutes. Finally, the family members slowly walked into the library, fearing they might disturb the silent environment. They found Thomas hunched over a book while sitting in his soft armchair, which stood at the back of the room.

"Yes, of course. That's it," he mumbled under his breath as he quickly slammed the book shut, rose from his chair, and rushed toward the three onlookers.

"These symbols around the edge are a type of cuneiform writing system. The artifact must have originated with the Sumerian people over five thousand —maybe even six thousand years ago. The signs and symbols can have many different meanings."

"Can you translate the writing for us, Thomas?" Declan asked patiently.

"Why yes. Let's have a look. *Mound...city...conceals... stones...appear...gate...invites...truth...reveal...zero...answer.*"

"Zero is the Key," Dalya whispered repeatedly and slowly to herself. "That's a similar message given by the cryptex, Declan. And here it is again."

"Yes, you're right. What message is this medallion communicating to us, Thomas?"

"Well, *the mound city* may be a reference to Cahokia, located at the intersection of the Missouri and Mississippi rivers. St. Louis, Missouri is home to several pre-Columbian farming settlements from around AD 1050. It is believed that these settlements were once populated by Native American tribes who migrated from all over North America, perhaps even from South America as well. Cahokia once covered six square miles, and at the heart its largest settlement, one hundred twenty mounds were built. The different people that settled there were of different tribes. Today, they are known altogether as *The Mississippians*."

"What were these mounds used for, Thomas?"

"Well young lad, modern theories suggest they were used by the wealthiest families as a dwelling. Their houses and gardens were built on the mound's plateau while the common people lived below. The largest of these mounds, named Monks Mound, is considered the largest earth pyramid ever made. In fact, at its base, it is the largest pyramid in the world, topping Egypt's pyramid of Giza. It is believed that at its economic peak, Cahokia's population reached over twenty thousand people, which constituted a complex society for its time. Archaeologists now believe Cahokia had been the most populated ancient city of North America at the time."

"Do the writings and images on the disc have something in common? And if so, what is the connection?" inquired Dalya.

"Like all ancient art and writing, there is usually a connection somehow. I believe the Sumerian writing is directing you to discover something at the mound city."

"What do you think it may be?"

"Well, I am not exactly sure, but I do have an idea. I believe you are to bring this mysterious medallion to Cahokia. Once you are there, look for Monks Mound. You cannot miss its enormous shape. Somewhere on or around the mound, on the day of the spring equinox, take out the medallion and use it as a guide of some sort. It is known that the sun rises directly over Monk's Mound during the equinox. Perhaps when the disc comes into contact with the sun's rays, it will reveal ancient scientific knowledge or secrets. This is the reason why you have come to see me, is it not?"

Only prudent silence emitted from the family. "Do not worry yourselves my friends. You can entrust me to guard your mysterious quest and to keep silent about the disc."

The twins responded with a hesitant smile, still feeling uncertain about Thomas. He continued, "Maybe you will discover some ancient principles about our planet, or even about our universe."

"That sounds fascinating, but what does it all mean?" Mr. Salk replied.

"I don't have the capacity to answer that question at the moment. However, if you will allow me to keep the medallion, I could analyze the object further and check my library's resources to find the answers you seek."

Declan and Dalya looked at each other with trepidation, and then gazed uneasily at their Dad for help. Mr. Salk stepped in for them. "Well, Thomas, I think the medallion should stay with us for safekeeping. There are certain people who would like to acquire the object at all cost."

"Oh, is that so? Hmm, very well then. I respect your wishes. There now, young people. Let's get the worried look off your faces, shall we?"

Thomas gulped down a glass of water. He cleared his throat with a few heavy coughs and asked, "Where did you find this beautiful ornament?"

Declan replied first, "We better not say, Thomas. We sincerely believe you'll remain safer this way."

"We did find it in a desert," added Dalya to soothe

his curiosity.

"Right, the Sahara Desert, no, wait...oh yes, yes, that's it...the desert of Qarahunge in the land of Armenia, the ancient nomadic site of worship for thousands of years."

"How, how...do...you...know...Thomas?" Dalya asked, flabbergasted.

"A long time ago, an Armenian colleague, who was also an archaeologist, and I traveled through Central Asia. On horseback, we rode through the Armenian countryside to find one particular site. A site, as told by nomadic shamans, that contained the *Secret of the Ancient Rocks*, a secret so important that even today only a few people in the world are aware of it. We asked around but were chased out of the area by disagreeable locals who thought we were invading their lands, snooping around where we didn't belong. In one instance, we barely escaped with our lives when a zealous band of marauders killed one of our horses for meat. While the desert dwellers divvied up the spoils, we frantically galloped away on our remaining horse."

"Did you find the information you were looking for, Thomas?" inquired Declan.

"No, lad. We did not. However we found out that...wait...one...moment—you found the secret! Your precious medallion is the Secret of the Ancient Rocks," Thomas reacted elatedly at his deduction. "It was said that there may be an ancient secret buried among the rocks, a secret so significant that it would change humanity as we know it. And here you are, in my home, with this distant ornament of the ancient past. How wonderful indeed!"

Dalya interrupted, "We think this golden disc is not from around here—shall we say, not of this earth. Is there any way to know for sure?"

"Come with me." They all darted out of the house's back screen door, walked out into the back yard, and entered a dark circular area. The yard consisted of tall California oaks, which had been planted close together many years ago. Now, the oaks, whose long leafy branches clasped one another, stood erect in a closed circle which connected together to form a leafy canopy. Thomas cleared the central area by carrying fallen branches and other debris away.

As the busy archaeologist used his fingers to briskly sweep dust and soil away, one could make out a double cellar-like door concealed before. Thomas then opened a flap on one of the doors and inserted a magnetic card into a small slot. They heard an electronic *beep* followed by a metallic *click*. Thomas stepped aside. A minute passed and the doors automatically opened like a shark's jaw widening before clamping down to consume its victim. Below, a dark cavern greeted the visitors.

"Why did we have to wait so long for the doors to open?" asked Dalya.

"To allow me to change my mind about opening the doors…just in case I need to immediately close them again if any unwanted folks try to enter. One can never be too careful, don't you think?"

"Oh, well that makes sense," replied Declan.

"Now bring the disc down here," Thomas instructed to Dalya as the doors closed behind her. The basement was another laboratory.

"All right, here we go," Thomas poured a special ointment onto the disc. With his pinky finger, he smeared the gooey substance methodically around the medallion's surface. After a minute, he added a fine powder on top of the ointment and then waited. They expected something to happen, anything. Suspense tugged at them as five minutes had passed. All of a sudden, a very faint vapor began to rise off the disc. Thomas carefully scraped the hardened chemicals from the disc and deposited the material onto a glass slide. Afterward, he sealed the slide with a small glass cover.

"Now, let us discover what the disc will reveal, hmmm?" He placed the slide under a special, high powered microscope. Gazing into the medium-sized lens, he wasn't satisfied. Thomas then pushed a button. A larger lens rotated and stopped above the slide.

"In all of my years studying metallurgy, I have never seen this kind of material before." Thomas lifted the slide off the microscope's platform and then placed it into a special machine for analysis. The machine swallowed the specimen Thomas inserted into its slit. It hummed for a moment until the contraption spit out a paper with technical jargon printed on it. Thomas tore it away and silently read the paper. Declan and Dalya, who were ready to explode in anticipation, eyeballed every move Thomas made.

"Is this really possible?" he slowly asked himself

aloud. "If my machines are functioning properly, which I assume they are, the disc's material is not from this Earth. In fact, the material may not even be from any planet within our solar system either."

"Oh my goodness, we are right about the disc!" Dalya answered.

"I think it's time we left. We don't want to get you into any trouble, Thomas," Declan suggested.

Thomas seemed startled. "What do you mean?"

Dad interrupted, "Thomas, thank you for all of your help. Sorry again to bother you on a Saturday." Dad and Declan shook Thomas' hand while Dalya carefully collected the disc.

"Wait one second. Allow me to clean the disc."

Dalya handed the ornament to Thomas. Methodically, he pulled out a bottle of chemical mixture, poured a small amount of it on the disc, and then wiped away the compounds with a sponge.

"There you go, young lady."

Dalya replied, "Thank you again for all of your help. We need to take the glass casing with us as well. The special metal on the slide should not fall into other people's hands."

"Why yes, of course, my dear. You have my cooperation."

"Let's go, Dad," Declan blurted out impatiently.

Thomas watched them exit up the cellar stairs into the sunny blue sky.

"Do you think they will remain safe, Thomas?" Ms. Blodgett entered the cellar from a second underground chamber just after the family had left.

"I think they will be fine. The children are clever and careful."

"I concur," Mr. Pascal added. He had also just entered the cellar from another chamber followed by Kate.

Mr. Pascal confided, "What do you think, Kate? Shall we trust them to use the Secret of the Ancient Rocks to reach the next level of their quest?"

"I agree with Thomas. They are cautious, bright, and also disciplined enough to accomplish the difficult tasks that lay ahead of them. They'll be fine, Michel."

"Well then, we shall move forward," Thomas ordered the rest of the group,

"Will SOUP try to capture the children anytime soon, Kate?" asked Mr. Pascal.

"No. At the moment, the consensus in SOUP's leadership is that they will not attempt to capture the twins for the time being. They want to monitor the children to determine what they will do next. SOUP knows the twins are on to something big. So they'll wait."

"Thank you for all of your work, Kate. We realize and appreciate the risk you bring to yourself. We are all grateful for your service to this cause," added Thomas.

"We're all at risk," Kate solemnly responded.

They all nodded to each other in silent affirmation. Ms. Blodgett, Mr. Pascal, and Kate walked out of the room through the two separate tunnels from where they had entered. Mr. Hipparchus exited up the steps and locked the cellar. As he thought about the twins, Thomas walked back toward the house where he decided to tinker with his flying machines.

✦

Spring Break had begun the day before visiting Thomas. The spring equinox was just four days away. The family's plan was to travel discreetly by car to Cahokia, staying away from the big centers and cities. They would stay in small motels or inns and pay for everything in cash. After a brief visit to Monks Mound, the family would then speedily drive back to California.

When the travelers were just three kilometers away from the mound city, Mom and Dad dropped the twins off before dawn. They briskly walked toward the ancient city while invisible.

"Hey, Dalya?"

"Yes?"

"I've noticed something strange lately since we've returned from winter vacation."

"Like what, Declan?"

"Well, my body sometimes turns invisible all on its own. Also, I've noticed a green glow around my body when the transformation takes place. It only lasts a minute or so. Have you experienced the same thing?"

"Yes, I have. Also, since we've been back, I've been having those dreamy visions more often as well."

Walking at a medium pace while vigilantly eyeing their surroundings, they talked intimately. Dawn approached in Missouri and already the air was unusually humid and warm for this time of year. A street cleaning machine nearly swabbed them with its rotating double brooms. The siblings leaped aside as the vehicle trundled past.

"Whew, that was too close," Declan remarked.

"Being invisible isn't as exciting as it used to be. It's quite a pain," Dalya sighed. "I mean, ever since we found that sinkhole, our lives are always within danger's reach."

"Yes, I understand what you're saying. Personally, I'm fine with the problems of being invisible. What really irks me is that we always have to worry about others wanting to get us because of our powers. It's just a fact of life now."

"I guess you're right."

The main boulevard leading up to the ancient city held no traffic or pedestrians during this early hour. The street sweeper couldn't be heard anymore. After a half hour, their path finally delivered them to the ancient mound city. Monks Mound, like other mounds in Cahokia, was built in layers of sand and clay.

"There are mounds everywhere! Look at the size of that hill over there! It must be Monks Mound," stated Dalya, excited.

"Do you know anything about Cahokia?"

"No, not really. Just what Mr. Hipparchus explained," answered Dalya.

"Would you like to learn more about this place?" asked Declan, willing to explain more.

"Sure would."

"According to what I've read, these fields were once

used for farming. Fishermen would bring in their daily catch from the Missouri and Mississippi rivers over there. People would hunt for deer and elk. The Cahokians survived on what the fisherman, hunters, and farmers would produce."

Yellow light streams started to stretch over the sky's blue-painted background.

"Declan, let's walk up those stairs to the top. I have a feeling that if the medallion catches the sun's rays from the mound's peak, we may discover something spectacular."

"All right, let's get up those steps."

The twins ascended the stairway which had been built during the past several years so tourists can have an easy climb to access the temple's apex. Their pulse and breathing began to quicken as their legs pumped up the steps. Finally, standing stiffly on the mound's plateau, breathless at the beauty that unfolded below them, Dalya slowly grabbed the gold disc from her jacket.

"I forgot to ask Mr. Hipparchus about these thirty-six notches around the circumference here," she stated in disappointment.

"I can tell you. I've read up on ancient art in Mom and Dad's old *Encyclopedia Britannica* books. The ancient Babylonians developed and used mathematics to build their huge towers and structures. They already knew about circles and divided the circle into 360 degrees, just like we are taught today in school. Only they did this nearly four thousand years ago. Today's Iraq was the Babylonian empire's land, between the Tigris and

Euphrates rivers where the Sumerians lived even before the Babylonians."

Dalya interrupted, "The disc has Babylonian and Sumerian impressions on it."

"They had already used degrees to map out the sky thousands of years ago. They studied astronomy and knew plenty about constellations."

"Do you think the Sumerian people learned math from the disc's makers?"

They both gazed at the object in Dalya's hands.

"I think it's possible, Dalya. Some scientists think that even Stonehenge's builders divided the geometric circle into thirty-six equal parts around the circumference before the Babylonian and Sumerian eras. Basically, no one knows who built Stonehenge, but some think it is dated over five thousand years ago."

"Five thousand years is a long time. Yes, I've also read about Stonehenge, how it could have been an ancient astronomical observatory. There is a circular rock at the center of Stonehenge that has thirty-six marks equally carved around its circumference, just like this medallion. The distance between each notch represented a ten degree angle. Ten multiplied by thirty-six equals 360 degrees, a full circle. It is said these markings were somehow used to map the stars' positions and movements in the ancient sky."

"Maybe this object was made for the same purpose, Dalya."

"Yes, but made by whom? And why was it given to us?"

"What I still don't understand is how it's possible that all of these ancient people built the same kind of pyramids, mounds, artifacts, and crafts all around the globe. I mean, there were no cars or airplanes back then so they couldn't just communicate ideas with each other in a short period of time. How is it that various ancient cultures knew so much about the stars, the moon, and the sun?" inquired Declan.

The dawn colors shined more intensely. "Wait, I believe the sun is about to show itself! Declan, let me hold up the medallion so the sun's rays shine on it."

"Let's hold it together."

Brother and sister held up the medallion, their arms stretching outward toward the sky. The last minute before the sun peered over the horizon was spent in quiet suspense as the twins waited.

Ever since the sinkhole discovery five months ago, the teenagers have searched for answers, answers that would explain the source and reasons for their powers. Maybe today, their search will end.

The sun broke free from its dark seclusion and began to push itself over the eastern horizon. Its rays shined directly over Monks Mound. Cahokia's eighty mounds revealed their smooth, grassy shapes to the world as the humps soaked in the morning light. Suddenly, the gold disc started humming in the twins' hands. Vibrating sensations began to spread throughout the twins' bodies.

"Declan, I'm not able to hold onto the disc any longer."

Just then, the disc began to pull itself out of the

twins' fingers.

"Let it go!" Declan yelled.

They quickly released the disc. It hovered vertically in place while shaking, then moved upward and away from the awestruck twins as a single sunray beam pierced through the center of the object. It flew quickly to a distant position two hundred meters away above the field where the single beam deflected off the disc at a right angle, contacting the ground.

Suddenly, the treasure piece shifted to a horizontal position, approximately thirty meters above the ground, the same height as Monks Mound's peak.

The twins felt an eerie stillness in the air. The fields and mounds began to slightly darken. Wind, bird sounds, crickets, and all other natural sounds came to a halt, resembling a total solar eclipse. The sky above was clear yet darkened to a deep blue. A translucent shield produced by the relic had surrounded Cahokia. No one outside of the shield could witness the event unfolding inside of its domain. There was only a small circular opening above Monks Mound. The mysterious artifact then slowly stopped rotating.

"Can you believe what we are seeing here!" stated Dalya, spellbound.

"Incredible!"

Suddenly, the artifact shot out green laser beams from all thirty-six notches. Each beam traveled in a straight line toward different points in the sky. The beams shifted around, stopped, adjusted again, and finally settled onto different destination points. After one or two minutes, a kind of Morse code rang out from the medallion. The beam from the disc's center shifted direction, shooting out toward Polaris.

All at once, the green beams began to shoot downward from their stellar locations to faraway places on the planet. The twins could see a grid of triangular angles forming in the sky.

Declan whispered, "Look at that. The Polaris beam is the thickest and brightest beam. Keep your eye on that one."

"Okay, I will!"

A second green beam streaked out from the center to form a hologram in front of the twins. Large green images played out before their eyes: a military ship, pyramids, ancient cities' remnants, henge structures, the first wheel, the Nazca Lines, and Qarahunge; all danced in front of the twins and then faded out, one at a time.

"Declan, that ship must be the one Ms. Blodgett described about Project Rainbow! All of the images have some kind of connection. They are the same images I visualize when my headaches start."

Just then, four numbers, in groups of two, appeared before them.

"Look, Declan. Those green numbers mean something. They look familiar. Hold on…those are the same numbers that keep appearing in my visions."

Another holographic image appeared. Declan pointed out, "Look there. Those are the same doorway markings found on the disc's surface."

Finally, the last symbol appeared.

"That symbol there is the Greek letter *omega*, meaning the end, the last, or the final part of something. The four numbers must be the coordinates which show the location of that doorway."

"Declan, I believe the letter *omega* indicates the doorway to be the final place to visit, where we'll finally discover the source of our powers."

"Let's remember those numbers, Dalya. The left one is seventeen and the right one is ninety-two which means seventeen degrees north latitude and ninety-two degrees west longitude. When we get home, we'll find the location in an atlas."

"How do you know it is north and west and not south and east?"

"Consider it a very good hunch," Declan confidently answered.

Suddenly, the disc's rays stopped beaming causing the hologram to disappear as quickly as it had come upon the countryside. Soon after, the shield dissolved. The relic automatically returned to its protector's jacket. Perplexed by the object's behavior, Dalya zipped her jacket. Safe and snug, the disc would stay inactive until its next mission.

Like determined mountain climbers escaping from an upcoming storm, the twins descended the mound's stairway. Disguised by their invisible powers, the siblings urgently walked among Cahokia's green fields.

Both experienced a premonition that the doorway held all of the answers they were looking for. The doorway was to be the final destination of their long, arduous quest.

What will the invisible twins discover at the secret doorway? Will their destiny finally be realized?

11 Temple of the Inscriptions ✦

Whoosh. The pages of the atlas turned quickly as the twins' fingers anxiously searched for the geographical coordinates.

"Dalya, would you let me look? Your thumbs are tangling up my fingers."

She abruptly withdrew from the atlas.

"There are the coordinates. Let's turn to the North American map, shall we?"

"Do you think we'll ever know why we are invisible?" Dalya asked impatiently.

"We are getting closer to the answer. I can sense it."

Declan noticed his sister feeling melancholic. "Hey, come on now. Don't feel discouraged, sis." He touched her arm gently and then hugged her.

She felt comforted by his affection. Declan was always the more positive one of the two. He always supported his sister through rough times or when she was just feeling down about situations. Dalya looked up at him, smiled, and rubbed his shoulder to signal him that she felt all right again.

"Now, let's figure out which location the coordinates show," Declan said, determined. They thumbed through the atlas and found the exact location and its name.

"Palenque, Mexico?" Declan continued, "Palenque is the site of some ancient Mayan ruins. From what I've read, Palenque existed from about 200 BC to about AD 1100, almost a thousand year span."

"Well, what happened to it?"

"Nobody knows exactly. Like other ancient people, they just vanished."

"Vanished? What do you mean by vanished? They lived close to a thousand years, and then they just suddenly disappeared?"

"That's right, Dalya."

"Incredible. Are there any theories on why the Maya disappeared?" Dalya prodded.

"Well, some scientists propose that they ate some bad food which caused intestinal diseases. These spread quickly throughout the population resulting in extinction. Some say the Maya were conquered by tribes from Northern Mexico who forced them to flee their cities and disperse. Over time, the Mayan descendents adapted to the customs of their conquerors. The Maya never regained their own territories. What is really amazing is how knowledgeable they were. They invented a sophisticated calendar that mapped out planetary positions and orbits, including the moon and the sun. Their calendar accurately calculated time periods up to 1,152,000,000 days! That is a huge number of days from a calendar conceived from long ago."

"It seems they were similar to the Babylonian and Sumerian people. It's that connection again. Common knowledge about math and science is found among all of these ancient people everywhere. How fascinating!" Dalya concluded.

Declan added, "It seems the more we learn about ancient people, the more we discover how similar they all were. For example, the great Pyramid of the Sun in Teotihuacan, Mexico is the largest stone pyramid in all of the Americas. What is incredible is that this pyramid's square base has the exact same measurement as the Pyramid of Giza in Egypt."

"No way," Dalya exclaimed. "That's unbelievable! Two separate cultures located thousands of miles apart have the same type of structure with the same measurements."

"That's right. There are other similar characteristics. The ziggurats in ancient Babylonia, today's Iraq, look more like the pyramids of Mexico than the Egyptian pyramids. Would you like to hear more?"

"Absolutely!"

"The Maya, Aztecs, Egyptians, Sumerians, Babylonians, and others could measure time very accurately. They didn't have clocks or watches or any other instruments that we know of at that time. Also, without telescopes of any kind, the Maya knew that Venus revolves around the sun in 584 days. With all of today's modern scientific equipment, Venus is now calculated to orbit at 583.92 days. How can they be so accurate?"

"You know what I think, Declan? I believe that some other people gave them their scientific and mathematical knowledge. And whoever taught them also knows about the source of our invisible power."

"You may be right."

✦

Spring transformed into summer while school had already finished two weeks ago. The twins had convinced their parents to travel to the state of Chiapas, Mexico. They flew to Campeche, Yucatán, and took a bus to Palenque, deep in the heart of Mexico. Transpiration already steamed up the early morning air as the jungle plants produced an abundant supply of oxygen, resulting in a heavy, humid mist. Sometimes it was hard to breathe efficiently through the muggy atmosphere. Heat maliciously penetrated the forest and its explorers' bodies as they inched along a winding, unpaved road toward the coordinates where the ancient Mayan ruins lay quietly.

They finally arrived at a local village about five kilometers from Palenque. "This heat is unbearable!" Dalya explained irritably. "It must be over a hundred degrees."

Dad looked at his watch, which rotated around his moist wrist. "It is 95 degrees. At least the forest canopy protects us from the sun's direct rays."

With rucksacks sticking to their sweaty backs, the family set out into the jungle.

"These mosquitoes are annoying. I must have a hundred bites on me," Declan complained.

An abundant amount of mosquitoes buzzed around

the group incessantly as they kept biting, injecting their needles into the hikers' skin to replenish themselves with their bloody cocktail.

"Well, it is to be expected. There are very few rivers in this region. Mostly, there are pools of stagnant water and natural wells that act as breeding grounds for the mosquitoes. Here, put some more of this repellent on," Mom instructed. The siblings anxiously rubbed the oil all over their exposed skin, hoping that somehow, miraculously, the insects would give up and fly away.

The family walked for two kilometers until they stumbled upon an old man with two donkeys. For a generous fee, the family convinced him to be their guide to the ruins. Mayan was his ancestry, and he was very knowledgeable of the Palenque ruins. He refused at first, but after their persistence, he realized the money was too good to pass up, and the family seemed easy to handle.

While maneuvering through foliage, around anthill mounds, and other obstructions, the expedition slowly stepped forward toward a clearing. Gradually, the canopy let in more sunlight, and the hikers pushed through branches that reluctantly revealed a beautiful, ancient stone city.

Three main temples and a palace dominated the city's central plaza. By now, it was early afternoon, and the stinging sun projected its brilliant rays down onto the dry, cracked ground.

"Excuse us, sir. Could you please tell us what these structures are about? I'd like to learn about that palace complex," Dalya inquired.

The short wiry man looked suspiciously at his visitors. He spoke gruffly in broken English. "You told nothing. I do not trust you my people's secret. You want only steal from mine."

The family eyed each other in full ignorance. What was this man saying?

Exasperated, Dalya exclaimed to her family, "We must be able to understand him. Time is running from us. We have to figure out a way to get more information. What do we do?"

Mrs. Salk tried to speak Spanish with the uncooperative man, asking politely and gently for him to describe the area. He simply shook his head and peered at the temple for a long time.

Declan then looked at his sister and said, "Show him the medallion."

"I don't know if we can trust him. What if he tries to steal it? Maybe he has friends lurking around the jungle waiting to rob us—"

Declan vehemently interrupted, "Just show it to him!"

Dalya cringed at her brother's unusually aggressive command, but remained cautious and hesitant. It was still her turn to protect the gold piece, and she took her responsibility seriously. The relic hung inside her shirt on a thick necklace. She thought the medallion would be safe on her body since she knew that one could easily be pick pocketed at tourist sites.

"Please sweetheart? My feeling is that we can trust him," Mom expressed sincerely.

"All right…here it is." She took the object out from under her shirt and showed the disc to the native guide.

Suddenly, the man's eyes widened as he now spoke fluent English, "Ah! You brought the artifact! You have been to the sacred desert and have found the *Secret of the Ancient Rocks*. It is indescribable to see the medallion here in my land.

Brown eyes squinted and eyebrows narrowed as the guide pointed to the largest pyramid and announced, "There is the *Temple of the Inscriptions*. Inside are the petroglyphic writings of the Maya and the Toltec people. You may find what you need inside the temple's belly. Over there is the *Temple of the Three Tablets*. Across the plaza, you see the *Temple of the Cross*, and of course, here is the palace with its three-storied astronomical observatory."

Upon hearing the man's words, Declan felt excitement coursing through his body. He had read so much about Mayan astronomy, and now he was standing right in front of the ancient structure from where Mayan astronomers observed the heavens.

"Follow me," the guide instructed.

Mom asked, "What's your name?"

"My name is Balaam. My mother gave me this particular Mayan name, which means 'jaguar.' According to our ancestors, jaguars were the protectors of dwellings and cities. My life's purpose is to protect Palenque from exploiters and thieves."

"Thank you for explaining your name." Mom won him over with her gentle demeanor.

The sweat-soaked travelers walked slowly through the center toward the Temple of the Inscriptions, the largest pyramid. Balaam stopped at the base in front of the main stone stairwell.

"Here inside lays a king."

"You mean," Mom inquired, "The pyramid is a burial ground for a king?"

"Yes, a priest king. The medallion you hold proves you can be trusted with certain secrets. Your presence here in Palenque with that disc did not happen by chance or luck, I assure you. Fate brought you here. Therefore, I feel comfortable enough to share my background with you. I was once a professor of archaeology at one of Mexico's most prestigious universities. You see, this iconic pyramid is the temple that protects the tomb of the sacred King Pacal. The Maya buried him below the pyramid's base floor. Most archaeologists now agree that the crypt was built first and the pyramid was built later around the sacred tomb to protect King Pacal's remains."

"How is King Pacal connected to the medallion?" asked Declan.

"Have patience for soon you will discover the answers you seek. Palenque was a forgotten city for nearly a millennium. In 1952, an excavation team found this pyramid which was concealed by the jungle's relentless growth. You can imagine how excited we were. We then discovered the entrance to the staircase, which leads down to the tomb. It took three years to excavate the stairwell corridor and King Pacal's crypt. At the top of the stairs, the team found six skeletons. One of them was a woman, whose job was to keep guard of the stairway's entrance to the tomb."

Dalya responded, "*We?* Who do you mean by *we?*"

"Well, nothing goes unnoticed with you, young lady. I will readily admit that I was part of the original team that first unearthed this tomb in 1952. We were the first people to enter the tomb since the Maya sealed it fourteen hundred years ago when Pacal died. One cannot describe the feeling we experienced from our extraordinary discovery."

"Why didn't you tell us this before?" asked Declan, feeling irritated.

"Well, certain people want to know everything about the original discovery. I believe not everyone should know everything we uncovered here. And honestly, I became quite annoyed over the years with everyone always asking questions about our findings. Think about famous people who always get bombarded by crazed individuals who won't leave them alone. At one point, we decided that some knowledge of this tomb would stay only with us. We resolved to protect the temple's secrets from the outside world and only give away its valuable knowledge to those who are trustworthy. You, my friends, are worthy of the Maya's secrets."

"Why did the work take so long?" Dalya asked.

"Well, archaeology is a slow and delicate science. Rushing through an excavation process could have destroyed a valuable artifact, skeleton, or other structure. The priceless information learned from these items would have been lost forever."

He placed his foot on the first step, next to the round sacrificial table.

"As I've declared before, you people seem trustworthy. Therefore, we shall go into the interior of that pyramid where you shall find whatever it is you're looking for. How does that sound?" Balaam asked, smiling. He began to like his curious followers.

"There is one condition, however. Only you two may come in with me. Too many people may disturb the chamber. Your carbon dioxide exhalations will damage the sensitive petroglyphs. The gas we breathe out corrodes the walls over time."

"Can we please go, Mom, Dad?" asked Declan.

Mom and Dad looked at each other, then cautiously at Balaam, who gave them a reassuring grin. "Yes, no problem. However, if you are not out within an hour, we are coming in after you," Dad firmly explained.

"Don't worry. You can trust me with your children."

"We'll wait out here and holler if anyone else shows up," explained Mom. "Would you be able to hear us from inside?"

The archaeologist assured, "Yes, but you must communicate from the top of the temple into the corridor, then we'll be able to discern your voices."

Mom felt satisfied. "All right then. Let's get started."

They all looked somberly up to the top of the pyramid in anticipation of what the twins would find. Balaam began his climb up the twenty-three meter high pyramid, followed by Declan, then Dalya, and their parents. A stone covered entrance loomed over them, waiting for their arrival into its rectangular mouth. Atop of the pyramid's upper platform, six pillars were built and evenly distanced apart. Each stone pillar showed Pacal the Great's family history.

Balaam whispered respectfully, "We have reached the entrance. Inside the pyramid, we have discovered over six hundred pictorial inscriptions, hence the name Temple of the Inscriptions. Now we will descend down the ancient staircase into the interior, where we will find King Pacal's tomb. What we will see here are original artifacts. Please be careful of what you touch."

Turning on a flashlight, he led the twins down the stairwell which was comparable to a diagonal tunnel. Crouching low, the adventurers moved slowly toward the tomb. At last, they reached the damp, humid chamber which measured approximately forty square meters.

"Here is the sarcophagus of the great King Pacal. The wooden tablet here is a thinner, lighter reconstruction of the original. A stone slab weighing sixteen thousand pounds used to cover this burial structure in order to protect the king's remains. This cover allows our workers to easily access the burial place. Tourists need to be satisfied, do they not? You can see the replicate engravings on it. The Maya were prolific artists. In my opinion, their artwork is unmatched by any other ancient culture."

"It looks so similar to the ancient Egyptian hieroglyphics," Declan stated.

"Yes, it is amazing how different cultures had such similar ideas. Let us take away this cover."

Together, Balaam and the twins lifted the wooden cover away from the sarcophagus. Empty space stared at them.

Dalya took the medallion out from under her shirt, unsnapped the chain's lock, and then held the relic in her palms. The disc began to hum and to glow, emanating a greenish haze.

"Look, the disc has started to behave like it did in Cahokia!" Dalya whispered.

"Why were you at Cahokia?" inquired Balaam.

"We just like pyramids," Declan answered, deflecting the question since he didn't yet fully trust the guide.

"One moment please." Balaam uncapped the top of his wooden staff revealing a button. He pressed it and a panel slid away. Dalya and Declan stared at Pacal's remains. His bones were wonderfully preserved by the skilled Mayan burial masters. The skeleton was lying at an angle on its side. Petrified leg bones bent to a half-fetal position while the skull rested on the left arm and hand. King Pacal's right hand loosely held a jaded spherical object.

"It looks as though King Pacal held the sphere rather close to himself. The burial workers from his era must have thought the sphere was important," Dalya ascertained in a whisper.

"My team and I thought the same when we first cast our eyes upon the king. The spherical relic must have some religious importance of some kind."

Dalya instinctually and carefully brought the glowing medallion closer toward the jade sphere.

"The Maya believed jade stones to be the most precious material of the earth, even more valuable than gold," the archaeologist informed.

"Look, sis. The sphere is also glowing!"

The two artifacts glowed intensely, lighting up the chamber with a greenish-blue pulsating effect. Dalya released the disc. Rising and hovering above the skeleton for a short moment, it floated slowly toward the chamber's far left wall. There, the disc placed itself onto a round impression, exactly its circumference. The medallion rested for a minute and then drifted away from the wall. The tomb began to shake slightly. Dust particles fell to the chamber's floor. With gaping mouths, the startled visitors observed an astonishing movement. The wall slowly lowered down. Behind it, a second wall revealed itself. Ornate illustrations and writings completely covered the wall while a green glowing haze engulfed the structure.

"Whoa, look at that!" Declan blurted out, feeling astonished.

"Extraordinary!" whispered Balaam.

"Obviously, the disc and Pacal's object need to be together to unlock the tomb's mysterious wall," Dalya firmly stated. "Can you translate the writings, Balaam?"

"I will try," he replied. The disheveled Mayan stepped toward the wall and used his right index finger as a reading guide.

Awestruck, the guide explained, "The wall reveals that zero is significant in the Mayan culture. It is said the mathematical concept of zero was given to them by another race of people. Zero is essential in calculating passage of time, the distance of planets and stars, food harvesting, and…wait…can it be possible?"

"What? What is possible? Tell us, please!" Dalya asked urgently.

Balaam added, "Empty visions, and…space travel."

"Empty visions must mean invisibility! Zero is connected to invisibility and space travel. The Maya may have already known about invisibility. But how does space travel fit in?" asked Declan.

"The answers you seek lay waiting at the Gate of Amaru Muru in the Valley of the Spirits in Peru. Go to the high place, to the doorway of Lord Muru. Zero is the answer. The rest of the glyphs, from my understanding, illustrate religious ceremonies, festivals, and types of duties the high priests performed."

Balaam paused for a moment.

"Wait a minute, what is this?"

Training his expert eye closer onto a small inscription at the upper left-hand corner of the wall, he noticed a description about the number zero.

"Fantastic!" interjected Balaam. "We know that the Maya developed the use of zero on their own. The ancient cultures of India developed the use of zero and algebra as well. But look here!" Balaam gesticulated with nervous excitement. "These are inscriptions showing knowledge of geometry and algebra. A right triangle, spheres, our solar system with eight planets, the moon! Look at this line. It points to the North Star from Earth."

"Why is that?" Declan asked, puzzled.

Balaam speculated, "The line must show Polaris' light path to Earth. Or…it could show a…a…perhaps an outer space traveling path."

"Do you mean a flight path of some kind?" Dalya asked.

"Correct. You would probably find more information about this at the Gate of Amaru Muru I mentioned before. Incredible, who would have thought there were hidden glyphs beyond the tomb's walls? Fantastic!"

Balaam felt exhausted. He sighed with relief and began to weep with happiness. Tears trailed down as he opened his arms like a person ready to pray to the sky.

"Why are you crying?" Dalya asked, concerned.

"My friends, you do not understand. For years, since my discovery here, scientists have suspected that the Maya had knowledge of the number zero. We just simply didn't know how much they knew about mathematics. Now we will understand more about how the Maya invented the calendar and used zero to calculate the great astronomical distances of our solar system and beyond. How genius of them! The world will be told about this remarkable revelation."

"I am glad you have decided to share your knowledge with the world. Humanity will be better off." Dalya lightly touched Balaam's shoulder as they both grinned respectfully at each other.

Outside, the temperature became hotter and more humid as the thick air reached one hundred degrees Fahrenheit. Inside the chamber, the thick, heavy air weighed down the visitors. The explorers had to make an effort to breathe in and out to acquire the scarce oxygen.

"C'mon, let's make our way out of the temple. It's starting to feel creepy in here," Dalya suggested.

"We should somehow cover this secret cuneiform wall before we leave," Declan said in a concerned tone. "Balaam, do you have any ideas?"

As a result of his findings, the scientist just sat in a corner in a joyous, dreamy state. The guide didn't seem to be aware of his surroundings.

"Balaam!" Declan cried out.

"Uh…yes. What is it?"

"How can we cover up this ancient wall? We don't want anyone else to view its secrets."

"I really don't know, young man. It's also the first time I've seen this wall."

"All right, fine," countered Dalya. "Let's just try to say something that might get this thing closed. Uh…close, *corer, credo*."

Declan interjected, "Wait a minute. Could it be?"

He then drew in a breath as he slowly walked toward the greenish-blue glowing wall. He stopped two feet in front of the structure. His eyes traced over every corner and all the cuneiform writings and symbols, and then he whispered, "NIHIL RESPONSUM."

A humming sound began to penetrate the chamber, while the secret wall began to vibrate.

"Bring me the medallion," ordered a resolute Declan.

"Here you are." Dalya handed the glowing relic to her brother, who clutched it tightly.

The unwavering twin extended his arms upward. The relic sat in his cupped hands. Suddenly, the outer wall slowly slid upward. It shut into place, stubbornly protecting the secret.

"Whoa…well done, brother!"

"Yes…very good," Balaam added with an awed whisper. He was beginning to admire these savvy siblings.

Declan handed the disc over to his sister. Dalya carefully strung the necklace around her head and tucked it under her shirt.

"Let's join up with Mom and Dad. We can then discuss what to do next," Dalya instructed.

Balaam pressed his staff's button. King Pacal's remains disappeared. The three explorers slowly ascended the dark stairway with Balaam's flashlight leading the way. Feeling relieved at reaching the top of the pyramid, they were blinded by a sudden burst of light. They squinted from the afternoon sunlight. Mom and Dad felt relieved at their reappearance. "Is everyone fine?"

Dalya unexpectedly winced in pain. She closed her eyes for a minute, grimacing while images repeatedly flashed in her mind's eye. Abruptly, all at once, the images stopped and her headache went away.

Dalya opened her eyes and instructed, "I think we need to go into that tall structure over there." She pointed to the three-storied observatory. "The building has important information for us."

"Are you certain, sis? How do you know for sure?"

"Trust me, I just do. Let's go inside and see what we find."

Slowly, the group descended the pyramid. They stepped sideways down the perilously narrow stairs while Balaam instructed them on how to avoid plummeting to the ground. "Do not look directly at the ground below. Focus your eyes on the steps. Concentrate on your footing as you support yourself with your hands."

They safely reached the grassy ground beneath them. Dalya immediately charged ahead to the observatory while the others hurried to catch up.

"Balaam, give me your flashlight," she asked.

The light darted around the musky, cavernous building. The astronomical structure smelled like an earthy mixture of plants, mossy stone, and animal urine. They slowly walked through the long palatial corridor to the observatory's main room. Upon arriving, the disc began vibrating again under Dalya's shirt, tickling her.

She took out the disc and waved it slowly around the room.

"What do you expect to find here, sis?"

"I don't know for sure. Something important."

Just then, the disc began to give off a pulsating greenish-blue glow from its surface.

"Wow, there it goes again," Declan commented, surprised.

"Look up there. You see it? There is a stone glowing on that wall. Boost me up, that way I can get a closer look."

Dalya then hopped up on her crouching brother's shoulders. Declan straightened out his body under his sister's one hundred ten pound frame, raising her up. She instinctively placed the disc against the wall. As the stone and medallion connected, the disc vibrated with greater intensity. Suddenly, the stone dissolved. In its place, a green gem revealed itself.

"There seems to be a button of some kind here."

"Press it and see what happens."

Without hesitation, Dalya pressed it softly with her fingertips. A humming noise could be heard on the opposite wall. The stone wall came to life. It inched toward them like a menacing monster and then abruptly stopped. The group did not dare to breathe. The wall then slowly lowered and revealed a metallic slab. Complete silence took over the room. Dalya hopped down from Declan's shoulders, desiring to touch the object. All five looked in awe at the metal slab which displayed gold etchings of circles, triangles, mathematical calculations, and diagrams of stellar distances.

"Look at that, would you?" Declan marveled.

Lost in thought, Balaam quietly muttered to himself, "Yes, outstanding!"

"And these calculations over here! They are showing the distance of eight planetary orbits. The zeros each have a doorway etched on them just like our medallion has on its surface."

"Declan, the slab must be a scientific record of some kind," Dalya stated.

"Zero is the answer…zero is the…wait a minute…Zero is the *key*," Declan whispered to himself. "I think I know what all of this means. Our medallion represents the number zero. As you can see, the Maya used the same symbol in many of their calculations. Somehow, they must have known about this medallion and used it as a zero digit in their astronomical calculations."

"How could the Maya know about the disc, considering it comes from Armenia? They never traveled to Armenia, did they?" Dalya asked, looking at Balaam for clarification.

"No, they did not. There is no historical written record of the Armenian and Mayan cultures ever being in contact."

The twins paused for a moment to let these new insights sink in.

"Let's go somewhere and talk this through," Declan suggested to a befuddled Balaam. "Is there a place we could lodge for the night?"

"Yes, of course. We can stay at a local village not too far from here. We'll sleep somewhere in the hamlet and leave in the morning."

"Let's go!" Declan said hastily.

"Well, what about the metal wall? We surely cannot leave it here for others to find," Dalya expressed.

"Hop on, Dalya." The twins carefully repeated the same actions they performed in unlocking the stone to restore the wall to its proper place, safe from tomb raiders and SOUP. The group exited the observatory and stepped into the late afternoon heat which felt like a spraying blow torch.

Tied up to a palm tree, Balaam's donkey had patiently been waiting for them. Balaam put a harness on it and led the group out of Palenque's compound and into the jungle toward a small, thatched hut village, a quiet Mayan dwelling just a few kilometers from the ruins.

✦

The travelers eventually arrived. Perhaps the village had existed in the jungle for over a thousand years. Poverty stained the village and surrounding countryside, yet the people were known to be very hospitable and generous toward strangers. The Maya and other natives of the region engaged in subsistence farming while earning small amounts of money selling their colorful handmade crafts and clothing at various big city markets. Filling visitors' bellies was an honor for the Mayan people.

The Salk family and guide ate well while chatting with the hosts. Balaam translated conversations well into the late evening. The Salk family was surprised and impressed at how cheerful the Maya were despite their impoverished conditions. They felt comfortable with their hosts.

A small hut was arranged for the family to sleep in. After the twins grew tired from the day's journey in the strenuous Mexican heat, the Salk family walked through a cricket-singing, mosquito-infested thicket to their open hut. Four hammocks dangled, swinging side to side from a slight wind. Exhausted, the twins settled into their hammocks first. Mom and Dad stood outside the hut, arm in arm. The twins began discussing their latest discoveries.

"Declan, if I understand what we saw inside the pyramid and the observatory, our medallion could be the original source for the use of zero. Is it possible? Or am I misunderstanding things?"

"No, it is possible."

"I still wonder how the Maya knew about our relic," Dalya thought out loud.

"The Maya somehow must have come into contact with our disc or they may have had another similar object hidden somewhere. Perhaps it might be hidden in Palenque."

"I didn't think of that, Declan. Imagine the ancient Mayan and Armenian cultures having the same knowledge because of this relic or another one like it."

"I think we'll find many more answers at the Gate of Amaru Muru."

"Tomorrow, let's ask Balaam where we can find this location. I really wish that finally this will be the place where we will find our answers," Dalya sighed.

The heat still hovered prominently over the village, not wanting to release its tight grip. A distant thunder interrupted the crickets' rhythmic chirping.

"Looks like all hail might break loose," Declan chuckled.

"You have a weird sense of humor, brother. There's nothing funny about tropical storms."

A villager lit a candle, placed it on the splintered wooden table at the center of the family's straw hut. The candle flickered, giving clue to an upcoming storm nearby. Swinging peacefully in their hammocks, the twins rocked themselves to sleep. Soon afterward, clouds rolled into the sky above, their puffy bodies settling above the village.

Later that night, they nearly jumped out of their hammocks, shocked by the sudden arrival of an electrical storm. As a result, the twins couldn't fall back asleep and lay silently in their rope mattresses, each contemplating about what is in store for them ahead.

Would the Gate of Amaru Muru be the final conclusion of their quest? Or, would the forbidden gate bring a fateful doom to those who seek its secrets?

12 The Chosen ✦

Crack! The wooden bat connected with the ball. Coach Whitney swung again with a grunt and another baseball sped along the inner diamond toward Declan's first base position like a shark speeding toward its prey. The ball took short bounces and rolled quickly toward the hunching first baseman. Declan concentrated while eyeing the ball with a hard squint as it kicked up dust during its speedy path toward him. The glove reached down, automatically pulling Declan's right hand with it and snatched the ball from the infield floor as the left hand plucked it quickly out of the glove's pocket and threw the ball to second base. *Out!*

The practice drill ended for now. Coach Whitney yelled out to the team, "All right everyone, let's take a water break before our running exercises. You boys look good today. I think we'll be more than ready for next week's game against the Titans. Declan, good pick-ups today! You are controlling the infield well."

Declan beamed with satisfaction and a confidence that he would do well against the number one team in their city league. It felt good to practice today, considering all that had happened in the recent months.

Overall, Declan was enjoying his practices much more lately. Baseball gave him a distraction from all of the thoughts that had been swirling around his head since he and Dalya had discovered the sinkhole nearly eight months ago. In seven days, the solstice would mark the beginning of summer.

He casually walked toward the dugout bench to retrieve his water bottle while chatting with his teammates. Coach Whitney talked strategy as they cooled themselves with drinks and shade from an old pine tree whose branches reached over the dugout and hung down just above their heads, reaching to scratch unwary bystanders with their needled fingers. Practice paced quickly along for another half hour before Coach Whitney blew the whistle three times to signal the end. Several boys collected their things and rode off on their bikes, homebound for lunch.

Declan said goodbye to the coach while the remaining teammates lingered and socialized. He hopped on his bicycle and began the ride home. His mind focused on Palenque. He began to go over the information they had gathered there and wondered about the connections they had figured out regarding ancient cultures.

A deep whirring sound slowly began to penetrate his inner thoughts. Gradually, the sound became louder and louder. Declan broke from his daydream state. "SOUP—they're coming for me!"

The bicycle's tires began to spin faster as the increasingly anxious boy pushed down on the pedals, adrenalin coursing through his blood vessels. A helicopter appeared over the horizon behind him. It was the same type of sinister helicopter that had loomed over them at the Eiffel Tower and the same helicopter that nearly stopped them in Switzerland. And it was now in relentless pursuit of the twin.

Declan hurriedly steered his bike into the nearby forest to escape. The deciduous canopy blocked the sun from entering, darkening the surroundings. He spotted a nook among some trees and hid. From there he could observe the helicopter. The machine came within a kilometer of him, its blades chopping up the sky while it roared forward. Then suddenly, it lowered and stopped to hover while four black-clothed figures clamped onto the cables and slid quickly down to the ground. They huddled for a brief moment and then separated while the team leader pointed toward Declan's position. Without further delay, they sprinted directly at him, barreling down on his location. The helicopter followed above them like a giant dragonfly.

"All right, here we go." Declan took his bike deeper into the woods toward a place he knew may give him protection from his pursuers.

The black hunters spotted Declan. One of them ordered, "There he is. Set your thumper guns on stun. We need him alive for questioning." The SOUP agents turned their infrared goggles on as they sprinted even more quickly. Declan pedaled his bike hard and weaved around rocks and fallen tree trunks and other debris that partly covered the walking path. Training his eyes on the forest, he looked for a pit he and Dalya had dug last year to be a hidden reading retreat. Overhead, he could hear the dragonfly roaring.

"There you are," Declan muttered.

One of the black figures ordered, "Let's split up. We each take a section of the forest. Now go!"

Declan rode to the edge of the hole which was covered by a camouflaged wooden lattice used as the ceiling for the oval trench. He lifted and dragged it a few feet aside. The bicycle belched as it crashed onto the bottom of the three-meter-long trench. Declan stepped down the rope ladder. With one hand, he reached for the lattice and dragged it over onto the reclusive hole.

"Kate, do you hear or see anything from your position?"

"Negative," Kate responded into her wrist intercom. "I'm still conducting a sweep of the forest's western side." Kate, not realizing she was a half meter away from Declan's hiding spot, stood with thumper gun in hand while scanning the brush. Her back faced him.

He thought, 'Our Kate…is here hunting for me?' Declan trembled out of fear of being captured and even more he trembled from feeling hurt and disappointed at this stabbing betrayal. Declan felt shattered.

He peered upward through the jailed ceiling above him. Maybe he was wrong about his friend. Maybe Kate was just playing out her role as the undercover operative working for SOUP. Wasn't that what he and Dalya had understood in Paris? But didn't Kate help them escape from the SOUP agents at CERN? Perhaps she had been fooling the twins all along just to capture them with their ancient prize.

All of these questions raced through his mind as his brain worked strenuously to process the situation. 'What should I do?' he thought. 'Should I call out to her and risk being captured? Or, was this pursuit her way of contacting me to impart valuable information while she maintained her undercover role with SOUP?'

Declan stood up and slowly opened the lattice to scour the area. He didn't hear any of the other agents. If he called out to Kate, then he must do it now before the others would come. Feeling very tense, Declan closed his eyes. His temples throbbed as his elevated pulse pounded though his body.

Kate began to walk away from him. Without warning, she twirled around, her gun in both hands, and shot a draft of air at the runaway. Declan suddenly gasped and ducked his head. He slipped and fell onto the pit's ground. The lattice shut with a quick *bang*! Kate crouched in a shooting position toward the revealing sound. Superbly focused, Kate inched in a knee-bent position toward Declan's hole while adjusting her goggles. She held her thumper gun chest high in front of her.

Her body's outline appeared just above him. She, unknowingly, stood a centimeter or two from the edge of the hole, not noticing the eyes fixated on her. The near frantic yet silent boy decided in a split second to call out to her.

Declan blurted out, stopping in mid-word, "Ka—" He then pressed the button on his gizmo. He quickly transformed into an invisible state.

"Kate!" he cried out cautiously, not wanting to be discovered by the other hunters. She then pointed her gun and shot a thump of air. The trees five meters to his right side received the crash of air and bent their branches at the full force of the gun's blast. Declan held his breath while he stood invisible with his head just under the camouflaged cover. He remained silent while evaluating what his next move should be. Kate stood still, ready to shoot her air pistol again at the slightest sound she heard. Just then, a deer crunched some sticks under its hooves as it quickly sprinted away from the human intruders. Kate swept her gun at the deer but held her fire.

At this precise moment, Declan flung the cage aside and slid out of the hole, crawling away quickly on his belly. Kate responded toward the lattice with a thumper gun blast. The cover lifted up and flew away as if swept up by a tornado swirling its deadly winds. Declan raced to a thicket of tall bushes. Kate scanned the forest. She found what she was looking for. A pinkish outline of a human body came into focus through her lenses. She pulled the trigger. Air blasted toward Declan.

Declan immediately rolled away from the oncoming rush of air. The bushes behind him shook violently. Kate swung around, preparing for another blast when suddenly her goggles exploded. Glass shards scattered everywhere. Kate suddenly felt something warm on her forehead. With her fingers, she touched her skin. A rush of pain surged accompanied by blood which slowly trickled down into her eyebrows. Declan had accurately thrown a rock that smashed her goggles. Now Kate was helpless in finding Declan's invisible presence.

Declan hid behind a tree. There, the twin found a sturdy, short branch and tied his rubber bracelet Dalya had crafted for him around the fork. He then combined a large, durable leaf with the rubber bands. A slingshot had been efficiently constructed. The twin picked up a stone and placed it in the leaf pocket. One other SOUP agent came running and found Kate hunched over in a dazed state of mind.

"Are you okay—" the SOUP agent blurted out. Before he could finish his sentence, his infrared goggles exploded just like Kate's had. A stone lay beside his feet. The man moaned in pain as some of the glass shards stuck in his eyes. He dropped his thumper gun. Declan sprang forward and sped past the two pain-ridden agents, plucking the thumper gun from the ground.

A parabolic shaped blast swooped toward the agents and flung them off the ground. The agents' arms and legs twirled and wiggled in the air as they flew backward and then slammed onto the forest floor several meters away from the shooter. Declan threw the thumper device aside.

The man lay knocked out while Kate struggled to regain her stance. A third agent stumbled onto the scene. Before the agent had time to assess what was happening, a rock flew into his goggles and smashed the lenses. The agent screamed out in surprise while frantically trying to pick the glass splinters out of his eyes. Another rock shot into his right knee. He yelped as he fell down, pain blistering through his eyes and leg. A larger stone crashed into the agent's forehead and knocked him to the ground where he lay sprawled in an unconscious state. There was one last agent out there somewhere. Declan darted around the forest vicinity with a cheetah's speed but couldn't find him.

A new feeling had taken over Declan. He no longer felt like the prey but had become the hunter. Just then, air forced him to the ground onto his back. Declan blacked out for a few seconds while the air left his diaphragm. 'He's above me,' Declan thought, gasping for air. Once his lungs were filled again, he leaped up ready to turn around.

"Stay where you are!" a steady voice chimed in before Declan could move again. "Lie down on your stomach with your hands and legs spread out. Do it now!"

Reluctantly, Declan followed the agent's commands. Declan's fingers were spread out. He felt fine powdery redwood dust covering the forest floor.

"We've got you," the agent announced triumphantly. "Now we'll finally have a chance to—"

Just then a cloud of dust filled the air between the two combatants. The pink figure in the agent's goggles disappeared. The agent, perched on a tree branch five meters above Declan, began to search the forest. His gun pointed and shot blasts of air in every direction. The thumps crashed into the surrounding brush yet none of the blasts found their target. All went quiet when the agent stopped blasting his device to assess his results.

Looking worried, the tree-climbing agent held his breath and eyeballed the forest. Suddenly, his goggles too exploded into tiny shards of glass.

"Argh!" the agent yelled out. Glass stabbed his forehead and eyes with its needled tips. He nearly fell off the branch but grabbed onto it with both hands. Desperately, he hung on as sweat poured from his forehead. Salt entered his glass-ridden eyes which made him squirm. A rock banged into his stomach. "Ugh!" bellowed the agent. The man let go and landed hard on his bottom. He sat bewildered at his predicament. His forehead burned with pain, a warm liquid ran down the bridge of his nose. A second rock torpedoed into his right cheekbone. The agent fell back, passing out. Declan examined the man and felt satisfied that he was no longer a threat.

Shortly thereafter, the triumphant twin tucked the slingshot into his back pocket. Then he approached Kate. She was standing now with a radio in her hand, preparing to communicate with someone. Declan stood in front of her, still invisible. He slapped the radio out of her hands. It landed on the floor between them. Repeatedly, he stomped on the threatening device while it smashed into bits, resulting in an electronic heap of metal and wires.

Kate observed the invisible force destroying her radio. She then backed off while her eyes were glued on the mangled radio. The forest was peaceful again.

"Why are you chasing me, Kate?" Declan yelled out. Kate's body flinched upon hearing his voice. She didn't respond.

"I want answers," he demanded of this mysterious woman. After having neutralized the other three agents, Declan felt completely confident, and he felt entitled to an explanation.

Kate finally responded, "I'm not really pursuing you, Declan. Please understand. I'm still on your side, but I must show SOUP I'm truly one of them. Otherwise, they'll begin to suspect I might be helping you. It's imperative that they never know about my true identity."

Declan pondered over Kate's testimony for a moment and then replied, "You were ready to shoot me when you had the chance. If it wasn't for my slingshot, I'd probably be a prisoner in your helicopter right now, on my way to SOUP headquarters."

"What can I say to make you believe me? You know, I had the chance to capture you when you were in your hole. You peered up at me when I stood just centimeters from you. I could have shot you; instead I intentionally missed you with my thumper blast allowing you to just barely clear my line of fire. My pursuit must appear authentic to SOUP. You've got to believe me," Kate begged.

Declan was not convinced. "I still don't believe you."

"All right Declan, I will tell you about what's really happening. As I've explained to Dalya in Paris, I'm an undercover operative within SOUP. I work for someone else, a special group that helps people like you."

Declan pressed his gizmo and then reappeared as a visible image once again. He stared at Kate, feeling befuddled. "What do you mean *people like you*? Who do you really work for?"

"Hold on, Declan. Let me explain. Maybe I can answer some of your questions. My job is to find and protect people like you who have special abilities. I work for SOUP because they, in essence, help me track and find these people. In addition, I'm able to monitor the other organizations out there who also want to discover people with special powers. SOUP is just one of many interested parties, but it's the most powerful and resourceful one. If I know what these groups are doing, then it makes my job easier to protect you, as I'll always be one step ahead. You see, Declan, I'm using their expertise and technology for my and your benefit. However, acting like one of them is necessary to not make them suspicious of my intentions."

Kate paused to allow Declan to absorb this information.

He stood quietly, still undecided if he should trust her. "Go on," he demanded sternly.

"I'm part of a worldwide volunteer network. Ten years ago, when I finished my university studies, I started working for the government. A few years later, an ad was posted for a unique job that involved specialized scientific work. As a graduate of molecular biology, I was interested and applied for the job. After being accepted and completing two years of training, I then became a trusted member of SOUP. Well, shortly before completing my training with SOUP, someone approached me about a very special assignment. The task was so important that only a small number of people in the world knew about it."

Declan, who was feeling impatient, demanded, "What's the secret, Kate?"

"You, Dalya, and other people have the same power of invisibility. We have recently found others just like you. It's no accident that you have these powers because you have been chosen. You are *The Chosen*. In the future, you will be asked to take on very important responsibilities."

"*The Chosen*? Selected by whom? We're just teenagers for crying out loud."

"I will clarify some things for you. Sometime in your future, you will be asked to protect one of the world's most important secrets. It's the secret of who the first humans really were and when they lived. The original or first race of people who lived on our planet was very powerful and technologically advanced. Today, the descendants of this race want to keep their identities hidden. They feel the world isn't ready to learn about them just yet. Their concern is that people will be shocked by the truth and that their powers may be exploited by those who want to use them for their own greedy purposes."

"Well, who are these 'first' people?" Declan gasped.

"In time, you will have all your answers. My superiors have asked me to only reveal limited information when it's absolutely unavoidable. I don't even know the full plan for you and Dalya. It's for your protection and theirs—in case you get caught by someone, like you nearly did today. Declan, you and

Dalya are part of a big scheme, a plan to protect a scientific secret about the human race."

The faint sound of a helicopter interrupted their conversation. Alarmed, Kate instructed, "You and Dalya must get to Peru and visit the *Gate of Amaru Muru*. There, you will finally come upon the conclusion of your quest. The helicopter will be here soon to investigate what happened to my SOUP team. The agents will ask me many questions about what transpired here. You must not tell anyone but Dalya what we spoke about today."

"I still do not fully trust you, Kate."

Exasperated, Kate responded, "My immediate superior is Mr. Hipparchus. He's part of the secret group that I work for. Ms. Blodgett and Mr. Pascal are part of our organization as well. Balaam, your guide in Palenque, also works with us. It's he who informed our group about the *Gate of Amaru Muru*. How else would I know about your next destination? Do you trust me now?"

The puzzled twin was overwhelmed with Kate's disclosure. He hesitated for a moment.

"Yes, I think so." Declan still doubted her slightly.

"Now quick," Kate instructed, "Help me destroy the other agents' radios. I'll need to explain to the oncoming SOUP team why I didn't call in for help. I'll tell them that you've destroyed all of the radios during our confrontation. My story must be flawless."

Declan and Kate then proceeded to aggressively stomp on every radio. The helicopter relentlessly bellowed forth its deafening sound. When the radios were all pulverized, Kate instructed, "You must get home quickly, pack your things, and get out of your house. They'll come looking for you there. Retrieve your parents and Dalya, and journey to Peru as quickly as possible. All of you must escape. Now get out of here."

"But Dalya is at school participating in the summer Science Club meeting."

Kate reassured him, "All right, I'll make sure one of our people will inform her to get home as fast as possible. No worries, Declan."

"Will we see each other again, Kate?"

"Yes, I promise we will. Now you must go!"

The twin collected his bike from the ditch, its baseball glove still attached to the handlebar. Declan rode out of the forest and back onto the footpath leading toward his home. He thought about getting home right away to tell the family to pack up and escape. But Declan's instinct directed him to find Dalya first.

✦

Meanwhile, Dalya sat in the school's science laboratory. Scientific posters hung from the walls displaying their cyclical concepts. One poster showed the water cycle, another revealed the carbon cycle. A botanical poster showed the cross section of a tulip. Another dilapidated poster hung loosely showing the human body's muscular tissues. The human skeleton stretched out its hands as the red muscles supported arteries and blue veins.

She and her Science Club teammates were talking

about strategies for winning the Regional Science Club Competition, which would take place next school year in October. Suddenly, Mr. Tesla looked toward the classroom door window and then immediately shot out of his chair. Someone stood in the outer corridor just out of sight. Dalya casually glanced over in Mr. Tesla's direction and noticed he whispered in an agitated tone. With one hand on the door handle, he leaned into the hallway as he and the mysterious visitor involved themselves in an intense discussion.

After several seconds, Dalya turned to focus again on the strategy discussion. Mr. Tesla, who looked flustered, walked back over to the group and announced, "Excuse me, gang, but I think we should take a break. Meet back here in fifteen minutes, and we'll go over what you've discussed."

Dalya and the other seven members began to file out of the laboratory discussing where they should take their break when suddenly Mr. Tesla spoke. "Dalya, could I speak with you for just a moment about the chemistry models you'd like to use at the competition?"

"Oh, uh, sure, Mr. Tesla," Dalya responded, startled at the abrupt request. "Go ahead without me," she instructed her friends.

"What is it, Mr. Tesla? You look upset."

Mr. Tesla eyed the door to make sure everyone had left, and then he fixated on Dalya. The wrinkles around his deep blue eyes revealed his ageing, late-forties complexion.

"Dalya, I have some news about your brother. He

has been in some trouble."

Dalya spoke with urgency, "What? Is he all right?"

"Yes, Declan is fine but was nearly captured by some people. He escaped and is on his way to your house."

"Okay, I'm glad he's fine. I must go home immediately to meet him…" The twin's voice trailed off and then stopped. She suspiciously stared at Mr. Tesla in silence and asked in a low cautious tone, "How do you know about my brother's escape?"

There was a pause of silence between the two as they both stared at each other, wondering what the other would do next.

Mr. Tesla spoke first. "Dalya, there is some vital secret information I'd like to share with you."

Slowly walking backward toward the door, Dalya glanced behind her to orient herself.

"Look, if you will just stop and listen to me, maybe I could help you and Declan."

"Help us? What do you know about us? Who are you anyways?" She frowned and looked at Mr. Tesla with a demanding posture while waiting for his answer.

"Well, besides teaching you science, I and some others were requested to take on a tremendous responsibility. We have been asked to safeguard our planet's most important secret. All inhabitants of our planet are affected by this secret, this responsibility…we, *The Chosen*, are burdened to protect."

The twin interrupted, "I've heard this before. What's the secret? I'm getting so irritated by different people telling me about this big secret and that I have something to do with this mystery. But no one has given us details yet. Just straight out explain to me what's going on."

The blue eyes glared at Dalya's face, examining her expression for a moment. Mr. Tesla replied after a slight hesitation, "You and your brother are part of an important group of people who will protect our Earth. Also, the truth about human origins on this planet will be revealed to you in Peru."

"How do you know about Peru?"

"I have been entrusted to pass on this valuable information to you at this critical point in your and Declan's odyssey. At this point, that is all I can say," Mr. Tesla insisted.

Dalya, who still felt flustered, complained, "This is all so frustrating. Forgive me for my rudeness, but why not just tell me about the secret of the human race's origin and also about the job I'm supposed to have instead of stringing us along with clues all over the world. And what's all of this business about the Earth being in danger?"

Mr. Tesla smiled warmly. "You and your brother will meet a special group of people in Peru. The people you'll find there will be unlike any other race on the planet. They are descendants of the first humans that ever existed, an ancient race that traveled and explored every part of our planet a long time ago. These ancient mariners are the ones responsible for building all of the marvelous pyramids, temples, and cities throughout millennia. They…" Mr. Tesla hesitated and then went on, "They are also intergalactic space travelers. This special group of people has asked others, including me, all throughout time, to protect their secret."

"You mean to say, that the first humans already had the technology to travel through space?" Dalya inquired in disbelief.

"Yes, they did."

Mr. Tesla stopped for a moment. Dalya remained quiet, contemplating the far-fetched information. "They want to organize the next generation of young people, like you and your brother, to safeguard humanity's secrets and to help them combat history's biggest threat to our world. From early on, I and other selected members were asked to seek out and recruit young people who would be trustworthy."

Dalya's interest peaked. "Why pick my brother and me? What makes us so special?"

"You and Declan are dependable young people with good values. You are bright and work hard in school. Both of you also show sympathy and concern for people around you. Since you were very young, you and Declan have always helped other students. You have spent many hours in our school's tutoring center to assist others with their assignments."

"How do you know all this about us?"

"We know a lot about your lives, Dalya."

"Why not tell the whole world about the origin of human life and the threat approaching us and our planet?"

"Well, you already know from experience that others want these secrets to conquer the world for themselves.

Another main reason is that if everyone knew about the threat, there would be worldwide panic. The world's various populations could become crazy with fear. Are you frightened at the moment, Dalya?"

"No, not really. I don't know what to be scared about other than that SOUP group who wants to kidnap my brother and me." The twin exhibited irritation at this thought.

Just then, Declan walked briskly into the room, panting from the strenuous bike ride. "How are you doing, sis? Have you experienced any kind of trouble?"

Declan rested his hands on his legs as he bent over to pause and catch his breath. He didn't notice Mr. Tesla at first, sitting on the edge of a lab table in front of his sister. After a few moments while slowly recovering his regular breathing pattern, Declan stood upright as he suspiciously glanced between Dalya and Mr. Tesla.

"What's going on? Why isn't the Science Club meeting here in the science lab like usual?"

"Brother, this is Mr. Tesla, my science teacher."

"How are you doing, Mr. Tesla? Pleased to meet you. I have heard many interesting stories about your classes. You have a reputation for being an engaging teacher. Dalya, we need to go."

Mr. Tesla responded kindly, "Thank you. It is a pleasure to finally meet you. I think I should continue with my explanations, Dalya, as we are pressed for time. Declan, Kate has already informed you about some items we are currently discussing."

Declan eyed them suspiciously. "Is that so?"

"It's alright, Declan. Trust me."

"You have my attention. We don't have much time, though. I just escaped from SOUP several minutes ago…"

"Not them again. Mr. Tesla just told me about you being in trouble. Are you feeling alright, brother?"

"Everything is fine, but we need to hurry."

Mr. Tesla continued, "Dalya, based on this magnitude of panic that would occur, both of you must keep this information completely secret. Please tell no other souls. Not even your parents should know."

The young girl looked guiltily at her brother. They silently eyed each other and nodded in agreement.

"Our parents already know about us and our powers. That's all we can say," informed Dalya.

"Well, we hope your parents will be very careful with your new knowledge."

"They will, Mr. Tesla, we promise," Declan iterated.

Cautiously, Mr. Tesla explained his ideas further. "The secret of our human origin is that we are not hundreds of thousands or even millions of years old. The planet is roughly six billion years of age. However, we have been around for only approximately twenty-five thousand years, a very short time in geological terms. Certain selected people have intentionally misinformed the public to hide this fact. Our forefathers already harbored sophisticated knowledge of mathematics, biology, and all of the other sciences we know today. They taught the ancient civilizations the sophisticated concepts of engineering, math, and natural science that shaped the pyramids of Egypt and the Americas. All of the ancient cities and stone observatories like Puma Pumbu and Stonehenge are the result of their teachings."

"Were these people also involved in building Cahokia?" Declan inquired.

"Yes, they taught the natives of America this knowledge."

"Where do these first humans come from exactly?" Dalya asked.

Mr. Tesla paused, and then he cautiously responded, "When you reach the stargate and open the stone door, there will be a group of people waiting for you inside. They will answer that question and fill in any other detail about what your responsibilities will be. You two will be among a select number of privileged young people who will be entrusted with the complete story of our human existence."

Declan urged, "We need to get home and tell Mom and Dad that SOUP is coming for us."

"Thank you, Mr. Tesla. We appreciate your help and everything you've told us. I'll try to be back soon to practice for the competition."

"Dalya, the competition is not important compared to the next adventure you must embark upon. I wish you two and your family all the best in your travels. Just one more item you should know. When you arrive at the gate, people you already know such as Ms. Blodgett, Mr. Pascal, and Mr. Hipparchus will be there to protect you."

Declan was confused. "Well, why will they not protect us on the journey to Peru? We are being chased with helicopters and guns. They've almost kidnapped us several times."

"Well, the tactical reason is this. To get to the stargate in Peru, you must first make your way to Tiwanaku, Bolivia. Once there, hire a local guide to take you to the gate. Tiwanaku is the last main stop before crossing the border into Peru where you will find the Valley of the Spirits.

A family of four is a common sight among tourist crowds and among people traveling to and from places such as Tiwanaku. A larger group of people, in your case at least three more, would draw more attention and suspicion. If you want to reach your next destination safely, you must maintain an ordinary appearance and keep a low profile. Minimize contact with others at every opportunity. Do you understand what I am saying?"

"Yes, absolutely," replied Dalya.

"C'mon Dalya, let's go," Declan gently commanded.

"Thank you again, Mr. Tesla. Please be safe."

"You two, be careful. Take care of yourselves."

The twins quickly exited the science lab and ran side by side down the empty school corridor toward the main entrance.

"I do have my doubts about Mr. Tesla. I'm not too sure about Kate's intentions either. We need to be careful, sis,"

The twins' running footsteps echoed off the empty corridor's red-and-blue painted walls. Bursting through the swinging glass doors, they ran into the brilliant sunlight.

✦

Back at the Salk's residence, Mrs. Salk busily practiced singing. She finished her last song and organized her notes when the phone rang. After hanging up, she walked over to the den where the busy architect was developing plans for a museum. Mrs. Salk placed her hand on his shoulder. Jolting from this surprise, he turned from his work to make eye contact with her. Mrs. Salk gazed seriously into her husband's eyes and firmly conveyed, "Mr. Pascal just called. It's time, Clayton."

The couple then walked slowly from the den into an extra bedroom. It stretched out to about four by five meters square. Relics from their past travels, paintings made by Mrs. Salk, and blueprints of previous construction projects adorned the room, giving it a cluttered feel. The sun's rays pierced through the window's old wooden blinds, highlighting the dusty air.

Mr. Salk took the classic dart board from its old brass hook hanging on the wall and placed it aside. Afterward, he opened a small paneled lid, painted the same color as the yellow wall paint, which exposed an electronic keypad. He briskly typed in a password and then looked silently at his wife. She nodded at him and approached the keypad. Mrs. Salk then typed in her half of the password to complete the sequence. She shut the panel and then placed the dartboard back on its hook.

Mr. and Mrs. Salk walked toward the room's center. Suddenly, a section of the floor slid open. They climbed down the dark hole on wooden steps to a cellar big enough to fit several adults. Dim lights had already flickered on. The basement's musky atmosphere greeted them. Silently, the two walked over to a special storage unit located at a far wall. The unit hummed steadily and quietly like a refrigerator cooling its contents.

The Salks repeated their password procedure with a different sequence. The unit's lid opened automatically while hissing vapors escaped.

"Let me," Mrs. Salk suggested as she eyed her husband. She reached down with both hands and took the small canister from its cushioned pouch. She held it up while a strange material swirled around inside, emanating a greenish-blue glow. The material inside are the tachyons Mr. Pascal showed them at CERN and the same material he had given to Mr. and Mrs. Salk during the escape.

Mr. Salk handed her a special carrying bag with a shoulder strap. Mrs. Salk carefully placed the canister into the mobile storage unit. She closed the lid, and it automatically locked its latch. Buttons blinked, giving information about the proper storage temperature, air pressure, and other stability features.

"Margaret, let's now make preparations for our departure to Peru. We have much to think about in the next days," instructed Mr. Salk.

Yes, Mr. and Mrs. Salk knew all about Peru and the reasons for going there. After the twins had arrived home, the family immediately left California and went into hiding.

13 Amaru Muru ✦

Vroom! An old bus revved its engine. The multi-colored vehicle snaked its way along the Bolivian mountains while its diesel engine roared loudly, pushing the reluctant hunk of metal along a thin road. The Salk family and the other passengers responded to the worn road by bouncing on their seats as the driver maneuvered the bus over the road rising to a height over 4,000 meters.

It was now June 20, five days after the family had left their home and just one day before the official start of Bolivia's winter season. The cold temperature was refreshing compared to the United States this time of year.

Unexpectedly, the bus stopped abruptly in the middle of the road. The driver called out in Spanish, "All right, everyone, you might want to walk from here. We are experiencing mechanical difficulties. I don't know how long it's going to take."

Many people sighed with disappointment, but everyone got out without hesitation, despite the spontaneous setback. While the Salk family contemplated their situation, the other passengers carried on as if being stranded was a common occurrence. Different groups of people walked to their destinations along the road and some on the footpaths that branched off while others decided to wait for the bus to be repaired.

"Unbelievable, we are stuck here. We'll never reach the gate," cried out Dalya.

"Well, we'll just have to walk from here. Let's use the map we picked up at the train station's news-stand. It may be a good regional map of this area," instructed Mr. Salk.

"What are you carrying there, Mom?" asked Declan, pointing to a bag slung around her shoulder.

"I must tell you about something. The case contains a canister of tachyons. We were asked to bring this material here."

"By whom?"

"Mr. Pascal."

"You've been hiding this material the whole time? Where have you been hiding it?" inquired Dalya.

"In a safe place at our house. Your father and I didn't want to add more worries and responsibilities since you two already have had enough to deal with during the past months."

"Do not be concerned about it. Now you and Dalya must finish your job here," Mr. Salk chimed in.

Off they went. It was early afternoon while the family walked along the main road for a few hours until they reached Tiwanaku. Arriving safely, they had found a small pension to reside in.

After dinner, they all gathered around a table. "Do you think this *Gate of Amaru Muru* is the final stop? For real this time?" Dalya asked, frustrated.

"Everything we have learned at Cahokia and Palenque indicates that our visit here should be the last stop in our long journey," concluded Declan.

"I guess you're right. We'll take our medallion to this gate and find out what is there. Maybe we will finally find the answers we are looking for."

"Exactly, Dalya. Now let's figure out what might await us at this gate, shall we?" Declan pulled out some papers from his rucksack. "Well, I've brought some information that I printed out last week. This article here says that the *Gate of Amaru Muru* is a stellar portal on planet Earth, a stargate or doorway believed to connect the Earth to other universes or other time dimensions within our own universe. Some people believe that space travelers arrive here on Earth through these portals. It is also said that there may be many more of these hidden gates located all over the planet. Yet the Peruvian stone structure is one of the few widely known stargates. The report says that some archaeologists think the stargate could be twelve to seventeen thousand years old. If this is true, the *Gate of Amaru Muru* predates nearly all other ancient sites."

"That's impressive. I never even knew that," confessed Mom.

"Well, for generations, the local Ayamuru natives have believed that the gate is authentic, and they still treat the location as a sacred site. Their legends describe the gate in this way: Thousands of years ago, Lord Muru and his wife came from another planet called Mu and established the city of Tiwanaku. Lord Muru was the god of science and warfare, and his wife the goddess of art, language, and all things beautiful. The Ayamuru believed that all knowledge came from the lord and his wife. Legend describes how Lord Muru and his wife traveled back and forth between Earth and Mu through the *Gate of Amaru Muru*. The Ayamuru also called it the *Doorway of Lord Muru* or the *Gate of the Gods*. They believe the location represents the original appearance of human beings on earth and the beginning point of knowledge."

✦

The next morning, they began the last leg to the *Gate of Amaru Muru*. An elderly guide had several horses for rent. Mr. Salk and the man negotiated over a fee to guide them. They reached an agreement for a fair price for three horses and the man's services. The third horse was to carry their rucksacks and other personal items. The family rode the other two horses the remaining thirty kilometers to the *Gate of Amaru Muru*.

During the trip, the family had enjoyed the spectacular geography the Altiplano highlands offered. Stunning snow covered mountain peaks rose to over 4,600 meters as vivid orange and yellow colors illuminated the nearby landscape of hills and flatlands.

"Whoa, whoa!" the riders gently commanded their animals to stop. All four travelers dismounted while the guide tended to his horses. Dalya chugged from her water bottle while staring at the rock formations looming in front of them. Suddenly, she experienced another headache while images of mysterious figures occupied her mind. Dalya imagined that she and Declan were standing inside some cavern while speaking with these strange people.

"We should be inside that rock structure!"

"How are we supposed to get in there, Dalya? That structure is solid rock," Mom stated, concerned.

"Maybe it's hollow inside," Mr. Salk proposed while analyzing the *Gate of Amaru Muru* with his trained architect eyes. It contains snake-like rock formations. One of them stretches from the lower left side of the rock and up over the doorway, ending its twenty-meter-long shape. A second snake-like sculpture starts at the bottom right-hand side of the doorway and extends diagonally about fifteen meters.

Dalya interjected, "I think there may be a way to somehow get in there. We must find a doorway and open it somehow."

Declan slowly took out the disc from under his parka and held it up. "All right, let's see what happens," he murmured as he walked closer to the gate. The disc vibrated gently, displaying a light greenish-blue glow in his hands. However, nothing else occurred.

"Declan, why don't you and Dalya hold the disc up together at the same time?" Mrs. Salk suggested.

"Excellent idea, Mom." Dalya peered into her brother's eyes. Both siblings carefully clutched the disc, extending the relic upward. Again, the travelers could hear only silence accompanied by the blowing wind. The family was puzzled.

"Remember Palenque, Declan?" Dalya felt intrigued and excited when she noticed a round impression in the rock face. She could feel her heartbeat begin to accelerate as she pointed it out to Declan. Declan approached the pocket. The medallion vibrated more intensely in his hands while the greenish-blue glow became brighter.

"Are you ready, Dalya?" Declan whispered intensely while looking deep into his sister's eyes.

"There's no going back. I'm ready," she whispered hesitantly, though she felt excited and at peace.

Just as Declan was about to insert the medallion into the stone socket a blast of air hit the surface right next to them, sending shards everywhere. The shock wave flung the relic from their hands.

"What's happening?" cried a startled Dalya.

She and Declan turned around quickly and examined the landscape before them. After a minute, three helicopters rose behind the next mountain range, ready for another assault onto the galvanized family. The pilots had been advised by the shooter on the ground. As the gunships flew closer, Declan's heart suddenly sank when he recognized a female in one of the front passenger seats.

He whispered to himself, "Kate? Oh no, undercover yet again? Is this for real?"

Dalya noticed the disappointment Declan expressed toward one of the helicopters, and then she also noticed Kate.

"Is that Kate in the helicopter? I thought she was

supposed to protect us, why is she with those goons?" Dalya asked, perplexed.

"I thought so, too," Declan replied. "It appears we were wrong about her after all."

Three blasts, one from each machine, lunged out of the helicopters' gun pipes. Dalya quickly plucked the relic from the ground and hid it under her sweater. She and Declan sprinted frantically away from the stargate, off into the distance. Dad ran off, searching for the shooter. The blasts missed their targets and pounded the rock face next to the Sun Gate. Dalya and Declan activated their gizmos to invisibility mode and disappeared from sight.

After several minutes of searching, Mr. Salk decided to rush back toward his family. Just as he turned around, the shooter jumped on him. They fought on the ground.

Meanwhile, Mom had found a safe place to hide behind a wall of rocks and decided to remain there during the confrontation since Mr. Pascal's canister needed to be protected.

"How are Mom and Dad?" asked Dalya.

"I believe they are safe. Mom took cover behind some rocks to the left there. Dad ran off somewhere."

"Knowing Dad, he probably went looking for the person who shot at us."

Another two thumps sounded from the helicopters. The usual lead agent was giving orders to fire. His keys jangled with each shot. The blasts hit the rock face, including the stargate. The twins hid together behind a rock formation while peeking toward the helicopters.

"They are not firing at us. They are focusing on the

stargate! SOUP must know about our interest in the gate. Therefore they want to destroy it!" yelled Declan.

"One would think they wanted to know its secrets, like we do. It seems they're only interested in our invisibility powers. If they succeed, the ancient historical secrets of humankind might never be revealed or proven to anyone."

"Or, maybe they just want to take the medallion to another location."

"We have to stop them from pulverizing that rock, Declan."

"But how? They probably have their special infrared instruments that can detect us."

The twins were certain they had to do something quick before the rock face was completely obliterated and pondered their predicament for a moment.

"Fire!" commanded the boss. Three more thumps whooshed into the rock face. A portion of the rock had already been blown away. The stargate's stony door was still intact but the rock around it was slowly breaking apart.

"Now let's retrieve the medallion and those pesky kids. Kate, you will lead a team to confiscate the medallion and return it to me. Pick three of our best men and go," ordered the leader.

Kate and three men from her helicopter hooked themselves up to the repelling cable and together sprang from the helicopter's platform in one cohesive motion. The agents zipped down to the ground, landing firmly on their feet. Immediately, they clicked themselves free from the cables. The four agents huddled for a meeting.

Kate ordered, "Switch your weapons from thumper to vacuum. We'll let the helicopters continue their assault on the rock while we pursue and capture the targets and their artifact. We only need to stun them. Is that clear?" The team members all nodded and set their goggles into place. Afterwards, they began their search for the children.

Declan spoke loudly to overcome the helicopters' roaring rotary blades, "We need to somehow take out those helicopter gun turrets."

"But how can we accomplish this when they can detect our invisibility?"

"We pick the right-sized rocks to throw into the gun pipes. If the rocks lodge themselves into the pipes, the blasts will not be able to exit. They might backfire and damage the helicopters, forcing them to land.

"You're brilliant, brother! Let's try it."

He picked up a rock, examined it, and then sprinted toward the helicopters. Declan ran at an extra-quick speed to get close to one of them. He held his breath and then threw the stone hard at the helicopter's pipe. It bounced off the pipe and flung away into the plains. He sighed in disappointment and then scanned the ground for another stone. Dalya threw a rock at another helicopter. It missed also, hitting one of the rotary blades which shattered it into pieces.

Just then, four beams trained on Declan. He hadn't noticed Kate's team poised for capture about twenty meters away.

"Ugh!" Declan groaned as the suction pulled him toward Kate and her team. He used all of his strength to claw the dirt floor but the earth didn't offer anything to hold on to. Slowly, he was dragged along the ground on his belly.

All of a sudden, a glowing electric beam zapped one of the agents, and he unconsciously dropped hard onto the floor with flailing limbs. His gun dropped and the suction weakened. Declan couldn't make out the source of the charge. A second agent buckled under a sharp pain to his head. A rock had smashed into the right temple. With only two guns sucking at him, Declan was now able to crawl away slowly from Kate and the other agent. He glanced over and noticed Dalya grinning from behind a boulder.

"Bulls eye!" she hollered over the roaring copters and vacuum sounds as she shook her fist triumphantly.

"Focus on getting rid of those thumper blasts while I concentrate on Kate and her team," yelled Declan.

Dalya turned around and leapt toward the helicopters. In midair, she threw a rock directly into the gun pipe of a helicopter. The rock slid into the pipe and then tightly lodged in the gun's mouth. The crew didn't notice the blocked pipe and fired another blast. The air backfired and exited the rear of the pipe, causing the helicopter to lose control suddenly. It whirled around uncontrollably while the pilot tried to stabilize his machine. The helicopter twisted wildly until it finally smashed onto the desert floor. The impact caused the men to become unconscious.

"One helicopter down!" Dalya cheered victoriously.

Declan smiled proudly at his sister. Feeling confident at Dalya's victory, the emboldened teenager turned toward Kate and her remaining agent, determined to escape from their clutches.

Off to the side, Declan now discovered the source of the electrical charge about fifty meters away up on a rocky hill. Mr. Pascal, Ms. Blodgett, and Mr. Hipparchus stood out in the open as each held a device. The group turned toward one of the helicopters and released an electrical charge from each device. Bolts contacted the tail rotor, causing it to lose control. As it descended toward the ground, its gunner released one last thumper blast. Ms. Blodgett and the others absorbed the blast's shockwave. They flew into the air, and then dropped hard to the ground. They lay unconscious.

"Noooooo!" Declan screamed. He frantically searched the ground for a rock with his trembling fingers. His eyes darted around the ground. Declan found a hard object in the swirling dusty chaos, clutched the stone, and then threw it toward Kate. The rock slammed into the other agent's stomach. The agent belched out a large pocket of air as he lost his breath and fell to the ground. After a brief moment, he recovered, scrambling to reset his vacuum unit on Declan.

All of a sudden, Kate knocked the agent out with a roundhouse kick to the head. The man flopped down to the ground a second time and fell into unconsciousness. Declan then slid toward Kate and stopped a few meters in front of her. While still pointing the gun at the twin,

Kate had clicked off the gun's suction power. Then she requested under the droning sound of the last helicopter, "Quick, Declan, hit me. Hit me now."

"What? I don't want to hurt you, Kate,"

"You must. Do it now before they get suspicious. Hurry, Declan!"

The torn twin was ready to strike her. But he couldn't hit her with his own hands. He hesitated, then picked up the man's blaster gun, switched it to what he thought was a low thumper blast mode, and aimed the wide muzzle at her. *Thump*. Kate cried out as the air wave knocked her down to the ground several feet away. She lay limp and silent.

Meanwhile, Dalya was busy hurtling one rock after another toward the last helicopter's gun pipes but not one rock found its target. The leader gave an order to the pilot and immediately three blasts of air trained on the twin. In rapid succession, the air balls quickly advanced upon their target. Dalya managed to leap into the air to avoid the first blast, and then landed on the ground and leapt again to out maneuver the second one. Both blasts slammed the stargate behind her. Dalya ducked under the third blast, however she was too late as the blast's circular perimeter just caught her right shoulder. Stunned, she slid backwards until she stopped near the gate.

Shaken up by the blast's force, Dalya moaned in pain. She felt paralyzed. After a moment passed, she could finally roll over onto her hands and knees to regain her strength.

The helicopter pilot kept skillfully steering his

helicopter right and left, forward and then backward, to avoid being an easy, still target like the other two.

Declan picked up a dagger-shaped rock. The weathered stone was about ten centimeters long and five centimeters in width. Its shape made it an effective projectile that could penetrate just about anything with just the right velocity.

Preparing to unload its next round of thumper blasts, the helicopter stopped moving around and steadied itself. "All right, get inside that helicopter and let's do some damage," Declan whispered. The unwavering twin took a deep breath as he tightly clenched the rock in his left pitching hand. Darting toward the machine, Declan focused his sights on the helicopter. Tunnel vision took over.

He cocked his left arm slowly back while shifting the rock into the best position for an accurate throw. Like reflexes, his fingers worked robotically. Every muscle in his hand strained as his fingers stretched to release the object at full force. Declan let out a "Hiyaaa" as the rock shot from his hand toward the helicopter. The stone sped on a straight path, right into the helicopter's gun pipe. The gunner pressed his firing mechanism. A small explosion erupted. The engine shut down right away, and the flying beast whirled around as the pilot tried to maintain control. The gunship struck the ground. The whirling rotary blades immediately broke into pieces. Projectiles flew in every direction.

Declan felt thrilled while he sprinted toward Dalya to help her get clear of the airborne debris. She crawled over a layer of rocks into a nearby ditch. Declan followed her.

Mrs. Salk continued to take cover behind some rocks while observing her children's courageous battle with the SOUP organization.

Rattling keys could be heard among the crew from one of the downed helicopters. A determined squint came over the SOUP leader's face as he scanned the surrounding area for the stargate. He quickly surmised the situation. The agent plotted his next move as he started jogging toward the family. His team members stayed behind to tend to their wounds. The SOUP leader put on his infrared goggles to scan for the twins. Just then, a swift powerful kick struck his backside, knocking him down. The thumper gun flew from his hands as he hit the ground. Mr. Salk surprised the winded man. Stunned for only a short moment, he instantly regained his composure and sprang up from the ground. He immediately began his assault on Mr. Salk.

A trained martial artist, the agent leaped forward and toppled Mr. Salk with a stiff kick to the stomach and an elbow to the chin. Mr. Salk gasped as the powerful chin strike knocked him backward. Mr. Salk landed on his side, hitting the plain's dirt with a heavy thud and lay still.

Horrified, Declan and Dalya witnessed the struggle from their ditch. Without hesitation, they rematerialized and then somberly climbed out and walked toward the SOUP leader, who now had his thumper muzzle firmly pointed at them. The twins stopped about ten meters in front of him.

Declan spoke, "All right, you win. We surrender.

We're tired of running from you. Do what you want with us, only please don't hurt our parents."

"Take us but let our parents and the others go, would you?" Dalya added.

The tired and weary siblings instinctually raised their hands to show their submission to the SOUP boss.

"Well, well. You've made a very good bargain. I want the medallion first. One of you, bring it to me right now."

"We better give it to him," Declan whispered to Dalya.

"Are you sure?"

"Just give it to him, sis," Declan interjected with a tone of defeat in his throat. Dalya looked deeply into her brother's eyes, then to the ground between them. She sighed as she took the medallion out from under her sweater. She looked at Declan one last time, hoping to escape somehow before handing over the relic. But Declan whispered, "Go, Dalya. Give him the disc, and let's just end this thing."

"You will come back with me to our base. I have other plans for the medallion and for you. Come on now, walk faster, young lady."

Dalya, who took her time walking toward the cunning man, began to feel disgusted at the thought of being in his captivity.

Helicopters could be faintly heard off in the distance. "They'll be here shortly. You have ten seconds to hand over the disc or I'll blast the both of you into unconsciousness like your friends over there." He pointed to Ms. Blodgett and her colleagues.

Dalya reluctantly took the disc from under her shirt and was ready to hand it over to the SOUP leader when suddenly the relic began to vibrate. It shot out from Dalya's hands and hovered above the twins and the agent.

Just then, Dalya took advantage of the distraction and lunged at the agent, ripping the goggles from his face. Immediately, the twins dematerialized again.

Declan picked up one of the downed agent's thumper guns. He blasted the startled foe. The air pocket slammed the man's torso. He reeled, twisted in the air, and fell to his side with a whack. The second group of helicopters was almost upon them.

"How do we stop them, brother? There are too many of them. We won't be able to escape!"

"I'm not sure how we can defeat them. We must stay invisible until we can think of an idea."

Just after Declan spoke, a ray beam shot out from the relic's center toward the sky and then spread out. A force field cloaked the area.

It was the same type of electromagnetic field the twins experienced in Cahokia. The helicopters halted suddenly. The greenish-blue bubble rendered everything within it invisible. The pilots could not fixate on their targets anymore, not even with their infrared technology. Thumper blasts tried to penetrate the shield but only fizzled out as they contacted the shell. Feeling bewildered, SOUP gave up the assault, retreating back to their headquarters.

The twins cheered in triumph and rematerialized.

The stargate was damaged but had survived the onslaught. Mrs. Salk left her hiding place while carrying the case. By this time, Mr. Salk had regained consciousness and slowly got up from the ground. The twins and Mom rushed over to help Dad. They all hugged, feeling grateful that all were safe and reunited.

Mr. and Mrs. Salk walked over to the weary, defeated agent and frisked him. Afterward, they placed his hands behind his back and tied his wrists together with a tattered piece of SOUP clothing. Using more torn clothing they had found, the couple then blindfolded him and tied his ankles, allowing him only enough flexibility to walk in short steps.

"Now we've got you," Mr. Salk remarked, satisfied. Restrained, the agent moved like a blind penguin with his captors over the Altiplano's flat ground.

"How about we take the agent with us inside of that stargate? If he remains outside, he may try to escape again. We don't want him to lead another assault on the gate," suggested Declan.

The parents looked at each other with concern, peered at their captive, and then turned toward their children.

"I don't know. If we make our way inside the stargate, he shouldn't discover the secrets we may find in there," replied Dad.

"Or, we take him and give him over to Ms. Blodgett and her friends after we've finished our visit inside the stargate. They'll know what to do with him," Mom suggested.

"We can try this idea and see how things go. Are we in agreement?" asked Dad.

Declan and Dalya stared at each other. They harmoniously answered, "Alright."

Dad grabbed the SOUP boss by the upper arm, guiding the man along behind the twins as they approached the stargate.

"Where are they anyways? I saw them get blasted earlier over there. But now they've gone," explained Declan.

"We are here for you now," Mr. Hipparchus replied, surprising everyone. He, Ms. Blodgett, and Mr. Pascal looked a bit tattered from their battle.

"Are you hurt?" asked Dalya.

"We are doing fine, Dalya. We've been in similar struggles before. It's nothing new for us," Ms. Blodgett replied.

"Well, well, you have a prisoner among you. Well done for detaining him," Mr. Pascal complimented.

Declan noticed Kate had just woken up. He went over to help her. "Kate, are you okay?" "Yes Declan, I'm a little sore but feeling okay. You did well." The twin helped her walk toward the others.

"Mr. and Mrs. Salk, the agent can remain under our guard while we are in the stargate so you and the twins can focus on your next task," instructed Ms. Blodgett.

"Thank you, Ms. Blodgett. Now, let's finally finish what we came here to do," Dad firmly stated.

While the twins were standing in front of the gate, the medallion lowered within their grasp. Declan plucked it from the air causing the shield to subside. Together, they inserted the medallion into the stargate's circular impression. It fit perfectly. They turned the mysterious gold disc counter-clockwise, and then slowly released it. The relic stayed in placed, independently attached to the round keyhole. Vibrating intensely, the disc began to give off a greenish-blue haze around the doorway.

After a few moments, both the disc and doorway disintegrated, leaving a deep black space.

The doorway hummed with an eerie yet soothing, pulsing sound that lured its discoverers inside.

"Take my hand, Declan."

The twins slowly stepped into the darkness. The doorway solidified once again with the relic attached to the door on the inside. Dalya retrieved it.

A dark abyss with swirling celestial objects such as spiral galaxies, comets, and meteorites appeared throughout the cavern, surrounding the visitors. A stony path lay before them, extending endlessly. Declan stepped onto the walkway first. In single file, Dalya, Mr. and Mrs. Salk, Kate, Ms. Blodgett, and Mr. Hipparchus followed. Mr. Pascal trailed behind with the SOUP agent. The path contained mosaic squares with ancient hieroglyphic symbols. An intersection of squares gave way to a stairwell that connected to a platform up high while the path continued on.

"We are supposed to climb these steps and wait at the platform," Dalya informed them assuredly. Declan and his parents looked at Dalya, unsure of her certainty.

"I've seen this staircase before in my visions. I just

know. I'll go first. Follow me."

Feeling confident, Dalya placed one foot securely after the other to begin her ascent while the others followed. With every step, the group began to feel more comfortable in this hidden realm.

"Isn't this beautiful?" Mrs. Salk gasped in awe, looking around while admiring the incredible images of nebulas and galaxies. "It's so peaceful and quiet here."

Finally, the whole group reached the platform and walked cautiously toward the center. The raised area seemed to be used for large gatherings. Two rows of stony chairs and a large stone table occupied the elegant platform which gave off an aura of nobility.

"It looks like an ancient Incan structure from Machu Picchu," commented Declan.

"Welcome, my friends." A calm deep voice echoed throughout the dim plaza.

"Who said that? Who are you?" Dalya inquired. Everyone looked around for the source of the mysterious presence.

"We are here among you," the voice iterated. "You all have done very well in your quest to finally arrive at our special place. Now you will have the answers to all of your questions, well-deserved answers, I may add."

"Could you please show yourself? We'd feel better if we can see who we are talking with," Declan requested.

A few moments passed while silence hung in the air. From the dark abyss, a few dozen people with white silky gowns walked onto the platform and stood nobly before the visitors. Different ethnic people were represented within the group. They were rather short and appeared to display a calm, composed demeanor. "We are a peaceful people and mean you no harm," claimed one of the figures. As if on cue, the hosts quietly sat on their assigned stone chairs.

"Please, sit down. We would like to talk with you and answer all of your questions," an elder stated. "Well, we see you have brought one of our foes. Let's remove his blindfold, shall we. He should fully experience what we will divulge here today."

"I'll do it," Kate volunteered. She untied the agent's blindfold and their eyes met. Disbelief transformed into hatred while the man stared intensely at Kate. She walked away and stood next to the twins.

"Before you begin your inquiry, we would like to request Mr. and Mrs. Salk to kindly hand over the case with the tachyons," said the elder.

Mrs. Salk had been clutching the case tightly throughout the entire confrontation with SOUP. She was hardly aware of how her fingers had gripped the case like a vice. Mom responded kindly, "Oh, yes. Please take the material. May I ask why you want the tachyons?"

"We only have a limited supply of the tachyon particles. We need the material your physicists have just created to maintain our stargates. Also, we need the material to travel between intergalactic ports and to create the force fields you've witnessed here today and before. Basically, the tachyon material acts as an energy source."

"You mean to say that you are some sort of intergalactic travelers?" Declan asked, intrigued.

"Kind of, Declan. We have the technology to travel great distances within our universe." There was a pause. "Using our stargates, we can travel to other dimensions as well."

"You know my name," Declan said, feeling surprised.

"We know all about you and your family. Now we must explain to you our purpose and plans that are in store for you here on Earth. Our spokesperson will take over from here."

A beautiful woman stepped forward. "Our story begins a long time ago. We are *The Mirifici*, the first human race ever to occupy this Earth. Modern science was able to accurately pinpoint where the first humans originated in Northern Africa and Mesopotamia, present-day Iraq. However, the original race of people appeared about twenty-five thousand years ago, not millions of years before like some of your scientists would have you believe. Compared to the Earth's age of six billion years, we people are quite a young life form."

"The shaman mentioned *The Mirifici* in Armenia!" stated Declan.

"Is it possible you are from another solar system or galaxy of some kind? I ask this question because Mr. Hipparchus here said that the golden medallion we found was made of metal not found on Earth." Dalya had many questions prepared in her mind.

The spokesperson stared back at her elders. Several of the group's superiors gave stiff, firm nods to her. She dutifully nodded in return. "Yes and no. We originally come from this world. Much later, we explored our galaxy and beyond. We discovered another planet we refer to as Second Earth and settled there. We cannot tell you the location of Second Earth. I'll explain why later."

"I find that truly astonishing; however, I have one question. We just discovered how to create the tachyons through Mr. Pascal's project at CERN. How is it that you were able to power your technology before?" asked Mr. Salk.

"Well, we had developed our own supply of dark matter on Second Earth, but most of the original material was stolen by a disloyal group within our race." The spokesperson sat down. "Now we must shift the discussion down another path, the source of your power and why you have it. Declan and Dalya, you have acquired your gifts for a very special reason. We would like to appoint you as the Earth's guardians. With this role, you will represent the new generation of young leaders we simply call *The Chosen*. You and others just like you have been selected to complete special missions. Among many other tasks, we'll ask you to enter top-secret buildings to retrieve important scientific information that could help us to prevent others from knowing about our existence. Your invisibility will help to achieve these and other operations quite effectively."

"Why do you not just tell the world about yourselves and answer the questions of where we humans came from?" Declan inquired.

The woman replied with a soothing voice, "Well, as your science teacher, Mr. Tesla, already attested to, we feel the world population is not ready yet to know the truth of its origins. And, as you know from personal experience, there are others who want to obtain our knowledge and powers for their own corrupt ambitions. Citizens like you will work to thwart evildoing in their own regions of the world."

The spokesperson made eye contact with the parents. "We believe that your children possess the determination and resilience to be part of *The Chosen*."

The speaker then addressed the twins. "You have proven to be altruistic with those around you. We have been monitoring your development since you were in primary school. Your parents have taught you to be virtuous, honest, and caring. You represent the type of individuals humanity can rely on for its protection. You have also demonstrated diligence, resourcefulness and endurance in finding this final destination. We feel we can trust you and your family to take on this responsibility in guarding humanity's secret of its originality."

Dalya interjected, "Thank you for considering us as part of *The Chosen*. Earlier, you mentioned something about dark matter being stolen. Could you tell us more about this point, please?"

The woman glanced back at her superiors. They gave their permission.

"Yes, very well. About two thousand years after we came into being, we discovered a way to produce the dark matter from the same metal you have on your medallion. A metal, our forefathers had brought to Earth from an unknown location. Our written legends describe the metal as peculiar and resistant to all other metals, rocks, and even fire. Nothing could scratch or chip it. Our forefathers secretly stored and studied it for centuries. Several hundred years later, our alchemists figured out a way to use it for the advanced technological purposes I've already described."

"I thought alchemy began in Europe in the seventeenth century. You already had alchemists?"

"Oh yes. Alchemy had already been developed since ancient times. Adding on to this, there is a bigger picture about *The Chosen's* responsibilities. You see, there was a splinter group of our people who plotted to steal the dark matter for their own selfish purposes. After a successful heist, the group then used the material to fuel its own fleet of very large spaceships, which could travel far from this world. They wanted to start a civilization of their own. With six ships' capacity to carry several hundred people, food, water, animals, and plants, over three thousand people left our settlement. Before they departed, their leader had vowed to return to conquer us."

Alarmed by what they heard from the concerned woman, the visitors paused and stood silently for a moment.

"Do we know when they will be back?" Declan asked.

"No, we do not know exactly. But our intelligence tells us they could return within the next three to five years."

Silence penetrated the platform.

"After their departure, we sent messengers to speak to all of our groups who had dispersed to explore and settle other parts of this planet before we left for Second Earth. Throughout the ages, we stayed in contact with our settlements on Earth. You know these people as Egyptians, Phoenicians, Sumerians, Indians, Maya, Aztecs, the Inca, and so forth. We sent knowledgeable people around the globe to teach these cultures about advanced concepts of mathematics, science, husbandry, and other technologies. Besides encouraging the advancement of human knowledge, the purpose of these teachings was to have each of these civilizations build observatories to track the heavens for us. You know these structures as Stonehenge in England, the Pyramids of Teotihuacán, Qarahunge, Cahokia, Palenque, and other observation points around the globe."

"So, it is true. Many scientists have proposed theories of what you just described. Until now, I never gave much credit to these ideas," interjected Dad.

"Yes. The purpose for this was for each civilization to plot and record the stellar coordinates we communicated to them. Each culture would use its observatories to keep track of our exact flight paths, flight dates, and landing coordinates on planet Earth. Throughout history, we've also operated this same strategy on Second Earth. Any deviations or additions to these measurements not communicated by us would mean that the rebel group would be approaching Earth. The stargates must be used sparingly because the dark matter is difficult to produce in large quantities. We don't believe the other group has the ability to travel through stargates yet like we do, but they can still travel at incredible speeds to reach planet Earth. However, we do not know exactly where they live." She paused and glanced toward her superiors. They nodded.

"Now, I would like to ask you a very important question. Declan, Dalya, we need you to help us defend this planet and Second Earth when the rebel group returns. Will you help us?"

The Salk family looked glazed over and didn't say a word.

"Please, you all need to think about this and talk it over. But keep in mind that time is of the essence. Let us know when you have decided. We will wait over here."

She joined her superiors and waited patiently.

Immediately, the family engaged in a discourse. After several minutes, Declan and Dalya walked toward the woman. Kate and the others stood silently in anticipation.

Declan spoke first, "We would like to know how many others from *The Chosen* will help."

The woman quickly responded, "You will not be alone. There are hundreds of others your age and with your powers who will be coordinating with you in the upcoming years. We will train and guide you to fulfill your responsibilities. We, you, and the other *Chosen*, will all be working closely together—this I promise."

"What do we do with him?" Dalya pointed to the man with the keys whose head pointed down at the platform in defeat.

"What shall we do with you, mister?" The elder

stepped forward inquiring with a firm tone. "Will you and your organization join us in this battle for our posterity or will you allow yourself and everyone else to be conquered? You must decide between your self-interest, which will lead to your demise, or helping us save our worlds and people."

Slowly, the stubborn agent raised his head toward the elder. A minute passed and silence persisted from the agent.

"What is your name?"

"Jeremiah," the agent answered proudly.

"What is your response, Jeremiah?"

In a cold tone, the SOUP agent replied, "I will put forth every effort to acquire the powers of invisibility, no matter how great the cost."

"Very well then, you will remain with us as our prisoner." They seized the belligerent agent and whisked him away.

Dalya and Declan locked hands and walked slowly toward *The Mirifici*.

Dalya spoke first with deep conviction, "I will join *The Chosen* and help our people when called upon to do so."

Dalya turned to Declan waiting for his reply.

"I, too, will commit myself to *The Chosen* and to help protect humanity and the Earth from harm," he said.

"Thank you, Dalya, and thank you, Declan. We are proud, honored, and grateful to have you with us. Let us come together and join hands to confirm our commitment with each other."

All of the tunic-laden people, the Salk family, Kate, Ms. Blodgett, Mr. Hipparchus and Mr. Pascal formed a standing circle and quietly joined hands in silence.

Each person was lost in thought about what would lie ahead. The twins felt especially proud, but also deeply concerned about their future. From this moment on, the twins' lives were once again changed forever. Declan and Dalya were now committed and felt ready to receive the uncertain fate thrust upon them.

About the Author

Born in Alaska and raised in California, Robert Guerrera earned a Bachelor of Science degree in Business Administration at San Jose State University. In 1993, he moved to Texas, where he earned his teaching degrees in Elementary Education and Secondary Social Studies at the University of Texas – Pan American. Ever since, he has been teaching Elementary, Middle, and High School students.

After teaching in the United States for several years, his traveling itch and curiosity to learn about different cultures led him into an international teaching career. He has lived and worked in the Dominican Republic, Mexico, and Switzerland. Presently, Robert Guerrera lives in Switzerland with his wife, two children, and his black cat, Lancelot. He teaches English, history, and geography at a private school, travels, plays the guitar, and writes.

www.robertguerrera.com

Made in the USA
Charleston, SC
19 December 2014